The Country Pirate

By
P E Alty

PublishAmerica
Baltimore

First printing

ISBN: 1-4137-8794-0
PUBLISHED BY PUBLISHAMERICA, LLLP
www.publishamerica.com
Baltimore

Printed in the United States of America

For my husband and children

Chapter 1
My Present Life

(The year is 1716, and the events that take place over the next few weeks are going to see a complete turnaround of Sam's life.)

Here I find myself again. Lying flat on my back in the long grass, staring at the clouds. Expressionless. Tired. The afternoon sun softly warms my skin, adding more color to my already bronzed and dirty complexion. A gentle breeze plays with my tatty cotton shirt, and teasingly flicks my hair across my face. "Is this forever what my life is to be?"

The cliff tops are so peaceful. I often come here when I am supposed to be running errands. The only sound that I hear is that of the sea below and the sea birds above. I close my eyes and spread out my arms, feeling the sharp blades of grass with my grubby fingers. If only this place and I could stay forever. The smell of the sea is natural to me, I know no different. I never venture more than half a day's walk from my home. Home—if that is what you can call it—I prefer to think of it as a temporary lodge. Yet I have never strayed from it for near 16 years. I know no other way. Too young to leave? Not brave enough to try!

Time drifts and I dream on. My thoughts are elsewhere. Anywhere, but mainly with my lost brother. I miss him so much.

The breeze has heightened and gives me a chill. It shakes me from my daydreaming sleep. Oh, no...my parents will beat me for being late again. The sun is now starting to set, I can tell by its position in the sky. I give one last glance to the mysterious sea. A twinkling blue, blending both sky and water. At least it is peaceful for the moment, when I get home all hell will let loose, and my parents will be like thunder and lightning, taking turns to strike upon me both with sound and force. But storms blow frequently at my home; it will just be like any other evening.

I gather the small bundle that lies at the side of me. It contains three large loaves of rough bread from the bakers over at the wheat fields. Ma always tells me to buy the cheapest bread from him, that is the loaves that are made with the leftover dough from the day before. Her guests, if that's what you can call them, won't tell the difference once its been soaked in some weak stew. I quicken my pace, as the sun sets further. Opening time will soon be upon us at the inn that I call home, so I run rapidly down the hill from the cliff and across the open country, to the bay.

As I near home, I can hear my Ma shouting. If she catches me coming back this way, she will beat me for sure. Quickly I hide behind the hen shed and manage to reach inside and take a few eggs. I will take them as a peace offering when I go in. With a deep breath, I stride over to the inn. Ma is waiting at the door, her face, as I had correctly guessed—like thunder.

"Where do you think you have been, Sam, we have guests? Guests already…and the stew is not ready." She flaps around like a sail that can't catch a breeze.

I hold out the eggs as an offering.

"And what do you think I am going to do with them? I can't put eggs in my stew. You know damn well that eggs are for breakfast. You are an absolute waste of time. No brains." She waved her arms around frantically as she spoke. "God forgive us for having to look after you. Get inside and make yourself useful, go and brush the room quickly. We don't want our guests to think that we live in a pigsty." And with that she snatched the bread from me…I got a belt about the head…and pushed in. It smarted for several minutes, but at least it was only off my Ma. If it had been off my Pa I wouldn't have been able to see right for the rest of the night.

I shuffled in to the kitchen, brushed the grass from my pants, put on an old apron and retied the tattered red scarf around my head. I took the broom from the corner—it had seen better days—just like my clothes, which were all hand-me-downs from my brother. I could never ever remember having something new for myself. He had been slightly taller and wider than me so everything I wore hung straight and loose. The pants had to be tied with an old belt of my Pa's. I trudged grudgingly into the inn's parlor.

Basically our inn consisted of three rooms with four doors. This was were it got its name of "The Four Keys" from. The entrance led straight into the parlor, guarded by the largest wooden door, heavily weathered, and locked by the largest brass key. The parlor led straight into the kitchen, via another door, smaller, but just as strong. The kitchen led into my Ma and Pa's bedroom, via a small door, and the fourth door led from the kitchen straight to the yard, which was mainly used for throwing the rubbish out. They all had their own distinct key to lock them. Four in all...all different. We had two full sets of keys; one set hung from my Pa's leather belt, and the other set around my Ma's neck on a large gold chain, which she tucked into her blouse.

The inn had not been originally designed as an inn. It had once been a wealthy fisherman's house. It stood not far from Calland Cove, whose waters led straight into the Irish Sea. The fisherman had disappeared, presumed drowned, so Ma and Pa seized the chance and moved in. Other folks didn't want to live in a dead man's house, especially one lost at sea, they thought his spirit would haunt it until the body was washed up.

The parlor was a self-designed drinking and eating room. Ma named it this as she thought it made it sound proper. It was set out with ten wooden tables and a selection of benches, all food and ale being served direct from the kitchen. There was also a large open stone fireplace, and four dark corners for 'dealings'. The food was cheap, and the ale was watered. Those who knew what to ask for could also get a shot of Rum, but Ma and Pa tried not to serve this as they didn't make as much profit from this liquor. But business was brisk, and it attracted all the wrong kinds! No questions were asked and nothing was ever seen.

As I stepped into the room, I could see that Ma had been exaggerating about the number of guests we had. There was only one. It was Old Tom from the village. Well, I say from the village, he really lived in the woods near by, a sort of tramp, unwanted and unwashed. He mainly came to The Four Keys for warmth and company. He never spent any money, but Ma used to let him stay as he acted as a sort of doorman, opening and shutting it whenever needed. At the end of the night if there was any stew left she would let him have a small dish full. So I took my broom and brushed out the room. Brushing away any signs from the night before, and Tom opened and shut the door as I passed to let me brush the dirt outside. When I had finished I retired to the kitchen, and placed the broom back in its place.

Ma was stirring the stew. A large cooking pot hung over an open fire, like a witch's cauldron. There was no great aroma arising as you would expect. This was mainly due to the lack of contents. Not only was the ale well watered, but the stew as well. A large pile of bowls and coarse metal spoons lay on the table near the fire ready for serving. It had taken me ages that morning to wash the remains of yesterday's offering away from them. We could get through over 30 bowls in an evening, and by serving cheap bread as well, my Ma and Pa made quite a tidy sum from what seemed a substantial meal. They always made sure that the guests had had plenty ale first though, so as to disguise the lack of taste in the food.

"Don't just stand there, Sam…cut the bread…mind make it thin…you know how to do it…lay it carefully on the serving plate."

I had my orders. Never a minute to myself. I was just a slave to them—not family. I picked up the large worn carving knife and placed it upon the first loaf.

"No!" screamed my Ma. "Like this…not like that…you'll serve all our profit away…Your brother, dare I mention him, was much better at this than you."

She snatched the knife away from me, narrowly missing cutting my fingers and proceeded to slice the bread herself. It was the same routine every night, she asked me to do it, then didn't want me to do it, and always compared me to my brother. My brother, whom I did not know where he was, had had the sense to get out of here four years ago. He was about my age himself then, perhaps it was time for me to go as well. But where could I go with no money. Sure Ma and Pa made loads, but where it all went, I do not know, for I see not a single penny. I am forced to sleep on some sacks in the corner of the kitchen and work all day. I wash, I clean, I gather eggs, I gather vegetables, I get water, I run errands for bread, I clean everything again, and I serve in the parlor.

My Pa returns. He has been to the village to buy ale, which he brings back on the donkey and cart. We can't brew our own here, so he does a deal with the local ale merchants, brings several barrels back each day, and waters it down. This is all he does all day, and he is always drunk, loud mouthed and crude. Then he serves it all away all evening, and so the circle begins again. Occasionally he will bring back several bottles of rum as well—for special guests.

The village is half a day's walk away, and no one from there except for Old Tom, dares come near us. We have bit of a reputation at The Four Keys for being a rough place where only the fool hardy dare come. It is true our guests are mainly robbers, thieves and pirates and others of that ilk. But my Ma and Pa are no angels, they can curse and swear with the best of them, and hold their ale much better. It is said that like attracts alike. Each evening brings at least one fight, and each morning sends away another several injured. I keep my head down, work hard, get no respect or wage, but keep my life and a roof over my head.

"Sam, Sam, were is that damned child?" My Pa shouts for me.

"Here Pa…just coming." I run out of the kitchen quickly and head towards my father.

"Take the donkey to some water, he has been working hard all day."

"At least one of us gets appreciated," I mutter in a voice low enough not to be heard. The donkey seems to be more loved than I am. I remove it from its cart and lead it to the fence and tie it down next to the bucket of water. I return to the kitchen, the night sky is now getting quite dark.

My Pa, although obviously drunk, still has the strength and balance to carry each of the four large barrels into the kitchen and sets them down on the floor. They are near to the door into the parlor, yet out of sight for when he starts to water them down. Ma goes over to him and gives him a big hug. They are both well over weight, and both very strong as well.

"Here you are, love, have a nice bowl of stew, and bit of the bread from the middle where it is still soft." She hands him a large bowl full from which she has drained away the water so it contains mainly potatoes and carrots. She also hands me a bowl, but I am not as lucky with the water.

"I feel a busy night tonight, love," Pa says. He spits out bits of food as he talks. Fragments spray over the clean dishes, but neither him nor my Ma make any attempt to clean them. "Villagers say there are two ships in port near the next town...crewed with rough looking sort of folk."

My Ma's face lights up. "We will need more stew then," she says, and ladles two more jugs of water into the cook pot, smiles and starts to sing softly to herself.

Suddenly Old Tom shouts out from the parlor, "Guests...guests..." and we all hear the front door being opened and shut several times. Here we go again!

Chapter 2
The Inn

Old Tom was busy shuffling backwards and forwards letting the guests in. The room was starting to fill quickly. The inn was ideally placed and decorated for our guests' needs. Needs which weren't much—just somewhere safe, to drink, eat, and usually sleep in a drunken stupor.

The inn itself was a long stone building, with a low slate roof. All the rooms lay side by side, one leading directly into the next. There were windows to all sides of every room, fitted with crude wooden shutters, which were surprisingly strong and sturdy when bolted. The parlor was the largest of our rooms. It was about half the size of the overall building. The front of the house looked westwards onto the cove, and the rear towards the fields and hills leading to the village. There was little protection against wind and storms, except for when the breeze blew from the north. Then the nearby cliffs saved us a little.

Ma and Pa had lived here at The Four Keys for the last 20 or so years, or so I am told. Rumor had it that the ghost of the previous owners haunted us nightly, and this kept the villagers away. But the only spirits that I ever saw were those that were being drunk, and the high personalities of our visitors. Ma and Pa feared no one, so a ghost was not going to prove any problem to them. I can't remember the name of the wealthy fisherman, and no one ever talks about him. I do recall, from when I was about three years old, finding a small smashed up boat at the bottom of the cliffs when out walking with my brother one day. But that could have belonged to anyone. A passing current had probably broken it free from its mooring elsewhere and carried it there one stormy night. Either way Pa gathered up its remains and burnt it as firewood the next evening.

Each of our rooms also has a curiously placed, very distinct, stone fireplace. The reason for this is not known either; perhaps the fisherman used to smoke his fish in the house and their curious positioning helped to disperse the smoke. All that matters though is that all three fires are fully functional, help us cook, and keep us warm in winter.

I can see from where I am standing in the kitchen doorway that Pa's handmade tables and benches are starting to fill. Old Tom still does a good job on the door. His hunched stance making him look humble, and his constantly twitching eyes not being able to look directly at them. His hands shake every time he goes to lift the latch, and he mumbles a greeting to them all as they enter. Most ignore him, but occasionally he gets an acknowledging tilt of the head, or wave of the hand.

Ma pushes me out of the way, and wafts into the parlor. She has put her best clothes on again. She puts her best, so she says, clothes on every night, but they all look the same to me. The crowd that is collecting stop their mutterings and rumblings, and glance towards her. There are several that I recognize from the night before, but mainly we get new faces.

"Gentleman," she calls out, "ale all round?"

"Aye," they all chorus together, raising their arms in the air in a cavalier manner.

"Coming right up…get your money ready." She speaks loudly and confidently. There is a sparkle in her eyes that she never shows towards me. The mutterings and rumblings continue, but a little louder. Ma pushes past me again.

"Out my way, Sam…go and get the tankards…do something useful instead of just standing there staring…come on now, hurry up." I follow her orders.

The tankards, which I also spent the morning washing, were kept on the large sideboard that stored my Pa's rum supply. It didn't look like a liquor cupboard. It had a false front, and appeared to all to be a chest of drawers, the type that you would store small linen items in, and knifes, and other kitchen utensils.

"Better out of sight, then out of mind," he would always say.

I picked up five tankards in each hand, just being able to wrap my slender fingers around the well-worn handles, and quickly trotted in the parlor after Ma. She had two of the largest pot jugs that you could imagine, full to the top with ale from barrel number one. That was the one that had the least water content in it. Once the guests had had a couple of pints from this barrel, Pa quickly starts to reload the jugs from the other barrels. Ma carried the jugs as though they were empty. I struggle to lift just one. She was a large woman, in every way. She had been raised with 14 brothers and sisters on a farm, and always said that her own Pa was too mean to buy a horse, so the family had to plough the fields themselves. Despite her size, she would weave expertly between the tables and benches and not spill a single drop, swirling and twirling her full figure to their delight. Holding the jugs at shoulder's height and smiling at the visitors all the time she reveled in their calls and whistles. She played them good. She was truly a master in this profession and would have milked them dry of all their money by the morning.

"Maggie Battle, thou are a sight for sore eyes. A full bodied and blooded woman. Come sit with me and drink my ale," a gruff voice shouted out. I followed as she headed for the table where she had been called. There, four men sat, so I left them four tankards and exited quickly without a word. It was my Ma's rules that she did not drink with any of them until all the stew had been served. She politely left them a jug, took their money, and ignored the slap on the backside that one managed to plant on her as she passed by.

After several trips to and throe everyone in the parlor had tankards and ale. I rested for a moment on a small stool by Old Tom near the door until the next round began. The muttering and rumblings were at their loudest, and intertwined with a wicked laugh now and then. It was never long before someone called for more ale, and I would go and retrieve the jug and take it to Pa in the kitchen to refill. Apart from me, the presence of my family was lacking, as Ma and Pa would keep themselves in the kitchen, peeping through a small crack in the wall every now and then. I think this was one of the reasons that our visitors liked it so much, there was no one watching and they could plot and plan about anything without fear of tales being told. If my Ma and Pa weren't there, then they couldn't tell on anyone if there was trouble. I was ignored, as no one would believe anyone of my age anyhow. My stories would get laughed off as youthful exaggerated tales. Not that I could hear them anyway, as they all sat in huddles with their backs to me. I felt lonely.

In drifts, my Ma would come with the first bowls of stew. The guests fall quiet one more time, and my Ma repeats her chant.

"Gentlemen…stew all round?"

"Aye," they chorus again, this time waving their tankards.

"Coming right up…get your money ready," Ma bellows out with delight.

I take this as my cue and follow her back into the kitchen. Stew and bread, I am allowed to serve, but my Ma collects the money. My Pa dishes up the weak mixture in the kitchen, and I start to carry it one bowl and one spoon at a time into the parlor.

"Maggie Battle…may the lord be praised…come work on my ship and cook for me." The same voice pipes up again.

Ma flicks her skirt teasingly in his direction and replies, "You old fool…the size of me…I will sink your damn ship and then you will eat nothing…just you a keep coming back to me here," and with that she snatched his stew money off the table, gestures for me to give him a good bowl full and blows him a kiss.

I often wondered how Pa put up with her obviously over-the-top flirtatious behavior; but then again she had the put up with his constant drunkenness. He was drunk now. Swigging the dregs from the ale jugs. But he still stood as solid as a rock. Just his complexion and slurring voice gave him away. He was also a larger-than-life character, over six feet tall and thicker than a tree. My own smaller-than-average stature must have been an embarrassment to them.

The serving of stew went on. Old Tom looked each time to see if the next one would be for him. But the inn was fuller than usual. So he would be lucky if he managed half a cup full tonight. A couple of the guests had shown him some pity and tossed him their bread. Or more likely, it was that hard they couldn't eat it and were really just trying to throw it out of the door. Either way Old Tom was always grateful for whatever landed near him.

The night rolled on. My Pa now lay out cold in the kitchen, having opened one of his bottles of rum, and my Ma had joined the partying in the parlor. There seemed to be no more secret planning, instead songs and shanties were beginning to be sung. Our guests always consisted of just men. Ma being the only lady was looked upon quite favorably, and I supposed treated quite kindly. No man had his way with her, although I dare say they were all wanting, but the others would not have let it happen. It was a sort of unspoken rule. They were here to fill their bellies and that was all! It was to be a good man's drinking night out.

This particular night, although busier than usual due to the two ships docked nearby, was to be what we would say a—very good and a quiet night. Come the break of day, all the ale had gone, all the stew had gone. Ma had a hidden purse as fat as a pig. The guests had cheered and jeered all night long. They had sung, drank, spit, cursed and only punched the lights out of three of the revelers, managing not to break any tables and benches in the process. I had long gone to sleep on my sacks before the last man had gone wobbling down the lane in the early morning light.

Tomorrow, or should I say this evening, it would start all over again.

Chapter 3
The Coin

So the next day had begun. I arose as usual. Stretched and straightened my clothes. I always slept in what I wore as that was all I had.

The kitchen was a very basic room. It contained little in the way of furniture, just the large sideboard as previous mentioned, and a large table to serve the food from, which also acted as a resting place for the dishes. There was a fireplace where the food was cooked, with an iron frame from which hung my Ma's cook pot, and a pile of wood nearby to keep the fire alight with. There were no chairs and nothing else but a couple of shelves upon which were placed a few small bunches of dried herbs for the stew, and a couple of odd pans. Anything we had of value, accept for the rum, was locked permanently in my Ma and Pa's bedroom, into which I was never allowed.

As I looked around the dim room, I could see that the fire embers were nearly all burned out. So I quickly placed some new logs upon them and gave them a gentle blow to try and arouse them a little. It was mid morning. For obvious reasons, we did not arise early in our house. I opened one of the wooden shutters on the window that over looked the chicken yard and the sun poured its golden rays into the room.

My first task of the day was to always cook breakfast, so I found a smaller cooking pot to place onto the fire and climbed out of the window with it. I was not allowed any keys, and my parents would not have thanked me for waking them so early. As the doors were always locked after the guests had gone, through the window was the only way out. Luckily I was small enough to squeeze through and had learned by experience to place a mound of the donkey's hay underneath to fall onto. Once outside I ran to the chicken shed, reached inside and managed to bring out seven eggs. I poured some water into the pan from another bucket I had filled yesterday at the stream and carefully maneuvered the pan, and myself, back in through the window. The entry back into the inn did not have as steep a drop from the kitchen window to kitchen floor as it did from the window to the outside.

The kitchen fire had got hold a little now, so I placed the pan onto the heat and waited for the water to boil and cook the eggs. While I waited I sorted the dishes into order for washing. Ma always cleared everything from the parlor into the kitchen at the end of the evening and then locked the door between the rooms. The eggs didn't take that long to cook, and I cracked and ate two myself, hiding the broken shell in my pocket from one, as Pa said I was only ever to have one. But what he didn't see he wouldn't know! The remaining eggs I left in the pan but pulled away from the fire so that they would not be too hard boiled for when my parents finally arose. At this time in the morning there was nothing else to do but sit and wait for them to get up, and then let them shout at me for doing nothing. I always found this rather odd, did they think that I was a magic spirit and could transport myself from room to room? If they kept all the doors locked, how did they expect me to get in?

After what seemed an age, Pa stumbled out from the bedroom. His complexion and voice were back to normal, but his stance and walk suggested someone still drunk. He staggered straight past, completely ignoring me, and headed for the eggs. He was just about to get one when Ma also came into the room. She was still wearing her best clothes...I don't think she had even got undressed last night...but she pretended that she had by imitating tying the laces on her blouse. The keys still hung around her neck, and she had a large key imprint at the top of her chest where she had obviously been lying on it during the night.

"Jacob Battle," she bellowed in her entertaining voice, "don't touch those eggs until I have counted them" Pa quickly withdrew his hand. She waltzed over to the pan and peered inside. "Five…right…how many have you had, Sam?" She tipped her head to one side as she spoke with an untrusting voice.

I showed her the remains of one of the eggs.

"Right," she said. "Can't those damned hens lay eggs in even numbers," and she whisked the pan away from Pa just as he was again reaching inside. Some of the hot water spilled on him. He cursed under his breath, gave his burnt fingers a shake and tucked them swiftly into his armpit to apply some pressure and soothe them. That was probably the closest his body had come to having a wash in years. Except for any spilt rum and ale that had missed his mouth.

Ma gave Pa two eggs.

"Why can't I have three, I am the man of the house." He thumped his clenched hand down onto the table.

"But who is it that does all the cooking and curtseying and organizing in this house?" Ma answered back, acting out appropriate actions to her words as she spoke.

"Aye,"said Pa. "Just this one time though mind." I laughed to myself. She said this to him every morning when we had an odd number of eggs. It was just that he was always too drunk to remember. She could play Pa as well as she could play the guests.

They both stood up while they ate, due to the lack of chairs, slobbering and slopping like pigs, dropping their eggshells on to the floor knowing I would have to brush them up. When they had finished, they unlocked the kitchen and parlor doors, and locked their bedroom. Pa exited the kitchen and headed towards the donkey for his usual daily trip to the village. Ma poked the fire to keep it going. The room was beginning to heat up with the sunshine from the window and the fire, so I quietly slipped out of the inn myself and started my chores.

A small babbling stream ran nearby. It was formed from mainly a collection of all the trickles from the cliffs, but with a hint of a natural spring for good measure. I took the spare bucket from the inn and generously filled it. I also splashed the water onto my face and neck to refresh myself. Heaving the bucket back to the inn, my need to escape this lifestyle came over me again. My brother used to do all the chores before he went missing. I didn't realize what a hard but carefree life I had until then. Playing all day and sleeping all night. The second he had gone, I was shipped straight into his place. Dressed in his clothes and treated the same. I was only 12 at the time, but expected to behave like I was several years older. There were only a handful of guests who noticed he had gone, and Old Tom of course. But after a couple of weeks his name never got mentioned again, apart from the occasional jibe from my parents in my direction.

Back at the inn I started to wash the dishes. All the cutlery first, and then the bowls next. The water in the bucket was beginning to resemble my Ma's stew, so I tipped it away outside and wandered down to the stream to reload. After three more journeys all the dishes and the large cook pot had been cleaned, and placed neatly back in their places on the large table. My hands were sore and cold from the water, so I tucked them up my sleeves for some warmth.

Next task was to feed the chickens, which took only a few seconds and a handful of feed to do it, and then I moved onwards to brush out the inn.

The floor of the parlor consisted mainly of large flat stone slabs. It reminded me of polished tombstones, intermingled with small patches of earth where the stone had broken away and been lost during cleaning…or fighting. In various places there was also a sprinkling of straw to mop up the spilt ale. It was like a stable. No matter how hard I brushed and brushed, the floor never came up clean, it just tidied. The stank straw was brushed at one side to be disposed of later when the main front door was unlocked. I straightened the tables and benches, and opened the window shutters to let some fresh air in and remove the lingering odor from the night before.

It was then that a small sparkle caught my eye. A flash of a twinkle, hit by the sun, and then gone. I was startled for a moment, and wondered what it was. I closed and opened the window shutter again to see if I could make it happen again. And there…a small speck of light shined back at me from a natural split in the wood on one of the table legs. I naturally went over to have a closer look. There I could see it. A small silver coin that had obviously fallen from one of our guest's coats, not making a noise on its decent as it did not fall onto the stone floor, but was trapped in a small nick in the wood. Completely forgotten about and unnoticed. I carefully picked it out from its resting place and I put it into my pocket, were it nestled amongst the broken eggshell.

"Sam…Sam…" called my Ma. "Come into the kitchen…I want you to go to the bakers."

Trying not to look like I was hiding my treasure from her, I walked neatly into the kitchen, keeping my arm pressed hard against my pocket so that the coin did not fall out. Ma had her back turned to me and was looking for her vegetable knife.

"The money's on the table, Sam…go and get three, no four, of our usual from the bakers. I feel that we will have a busy night again. Your Pa has already left for the village with the donkey so you will have to run down the lane on your own." She waived her now found knife at the table, then at me and then at the door, still without turning around. On the table there were eight silver coins, exactly the same as the one that I had just found. I picked them up casually, placed them in my other pocket, and headed towards the door.

"Sam!" growled Ma. Oh, no, had she seen through me, had she worked out that I was hiding something. She headed towards me. I froze for a second, then decided I was not going to hang around, and made a run for it.

"Bye, Ma," I called and ran as fast as I could with one arm still pinned to my side. Ma shouted after me not to dally, and raised and dropped her hands and arms in front of her gesticulating as though her request was in vain.

Out of sight of the inn, I slowed and turned off the road and headed over the fields towards the bakers. It was a much nicer route, but not a quicker one as I always started to daydream when I went this way. I remembered the coin in my pocket, stopped and took it out. It was only small. I had heard these coins before in the inn being referred to as pieces of eight. There was some writing on it, but being uneducated in letters I don't know what it said, but either way it was now mine. I started to walk towards the bakers again. What should I do with it? If my Ma caught me, she would accuse me of stealing from her and beat me with the broom. If my Pa caught me, he would also accuse me of stealing, and beat me with his fists. I had seen it happen to my brother in the past when he had helped himself to some of the guest's bread because he had had nothing to eat all day and was hungry. I had better get rid of it as soon as possible.

Presently I arrived at the bakers. There was always a delicious aroma here. The baker himself was a well-fed, rotund, well-spoken man, respected in the village. He had a lovely plump wife and three small plump children. The eldest child was about five, and they were always to be seen playing in the yard behind the shop with a wooden ball, chased by two small dogs, a cat and a friendly goose. I'd only had pebbles and grass to play with when I was young. Still despite his pleasantness, he would not serve me through the main door, and I always had to go around the back. I handed him the eight coins, and he disappeared into the bakery. When he came back, he had with him four large rough loaves wrapped in a piece of old clothe.

"When is your Ma going to give me some proper currency instead of this foreign stuff?" he asked. "Tell her it's about time she got a honest living and earned a honest coin...these silver things give me no end of trouble trying to shift them." But still he took them, and I am sure that he didn't get rid of them at a loss!

"Thank you," I said politely and took the bread. Just then his wife walked past with a large tray full of fresh baked buns. They looked perfect and smelt like heaven. I felt the coin in my pocket, what a perfect way to get rid of it. I knew that the baker would accept this currency and if I ate the evidence then my Ma would have nothing to chastise me about.

"Please, sir," I asked, "may I have one of those?" and I pointed towards the buns.

The baker laughed. "And what do you expect to pay for it with...fresh air and a smile?"

I pulled the coin out and showed it to the baker. His face changed shape and he looked a little uneasy. Looking all around to see that no one was watching again, he took the coin and disappeared inside. When he returned, he had in his hand one freshly baked bun.

"Now go, Sam. I don't want to see you again today. Your family will ruin my business..." He continued to mutter as he quickly closed the door on me.

I looked at the fresh baked, still warm bun in my hand. Guilt flooded my body—but greed overtook. I ran away from the baker's, my teeth tearing at the flesh of the product in my hand. I had never eaten anything so godlike before in my life. I was a changed person. I had seen a small glimpse of other things.

That day I went straight back to the inn instead of daydreaming on the cliffs. The evidence was all gone, properly hidden in my stomach. Surely there must be more. I must look for more coins. And it is from this that I decided to hatch a plan to get myself away from The Four Keys forever.

Chapter 4

Searching

Back at the inn, Ma was asleep flat on her back on the stone floor. She was laid out like a corpse at an undertakers with her arms crossed against her chest, and her skin was so pale in color that she really looked as if she was dead. Except for occasional facial expressions to produce a snuffle and a grunt, she lay mainly stone still. Every now and then though her fingers would twitch as though she checking that the keys were still around her neck. She always slept for about an hour before she began to cook her stew. Pa wasn't in. He was in the village, no doubt topping up his drunken state, and buying more ale for the night's activities.

I crept quietly past. She would not be expecting me back yet from the baker's, so I was going to make the most of my time alone and search. I was going to search every corner of that parlor. I was going to search every little split of wood on the furniture. I was going to search through the ashes in the fire. I was going to search and reach up to all the supporting beams and feel all odd bits of stone wall that stuck out. I was adamant that I would find more.

Carefully I went to the door. It opened inwards towards the kitchen, and when I squeezed and turned the latch it made no noise. I was pleased. But the hinges creaked. I always knew that they did, but when you want it to be quiet it always appears to be ten times louder. "Heeeeere," they said eerily as I pushed it slowly open. "Ahhh," they sighed as I pulled it gently shut, lowering its tone as the door became closer to closing. I turned the latch again, and gratefully once more it made no noise. Where should I start to search?

I decided to start at the bottom and work up. Floor to roof. As an alibi I had brought in the broom with me from the kitchen and propped it against the door, so that if Ma woke and entered it would fall and give a second of a warning to me. Bending my legs I assumed a crouched position and started to sweep my hands over the floor. The center of the floor was easy to see because of the light from the open window, but corners and edges were not as easy. I could not move any of the furniture because it was too heavy, and in dragging it across the stone floor its noise may have awoken the sleeping beast in the next room. I felt frantically around all the legs and bases of the furniture. A few house spiders ran from their hiding places and gave me a start. But after a good 15 minutes of feeling, all I had located was one black button. The tables and benches yielded nothing accept for one dirty grey handkerchief, and the walls gave nothing away either. To search the beams I would have to stand on the tables.

The beams were made of the largest, square pieces of wood that you could imagine. I don't think that they had come from local trees, due to their vastness in length with a continued equal thickness all the way. They were too high for me to actually see onto, but if I stretched out my arm it just gave me enough height to feel on top with the tips of my fingers. I was still desperate to find something. I had decided not to bother searching the ashes, as it would have been a fool who had thrown his money into the fire. So I climbed upon a table. Balancing on tiptoes I edged along, feeling with first my right hand on one side, and then my left hand on the other. Stretched to my limited I could just reach sufficiently. The dust was thick up here and frequently fell into my eyes and onto my head. I moved nimbly from one table to the next to enable me to reach all the beams. Then just as I was giving up hope, at the fourth and final beam I felt something. Carefully I removed it and saw that it had yielded a small round stone. It was shiny. About the size of a large pea, it was deep red in color and it sparkled when I held it up to the light. But this is not what I wanted. I wanted coins. I needed money. If I was ever to get away from here I needed to be able to support myself for at least part of my journey.

Disappointed, I stuck the stone into my pocket and forgot about it. I quickly blew the dust that had landed on the tables onto the floor and picked up the broom. Just in time. My Ma had awaken and barged in through the door. Her cloth cap was on crooked and her hair was messy.

"Sam, you useless piece of nothing. Just look at the state of this floor. It is covered in dust. Get it cleaned instantly." She flapped around as she spoke, urgency in everything as though her life depended upon it. She failed to notice that I too was covered in dust. The fact that I stood with my back to the open window must have silhouetted me against the daylight. She went back into the kitchen.

I removed my headscarf and shook the dust from it. The ends of my long brown hair were also covered in dust, so I removed them from the tie and shook them as well. I retied my hair, placed my headscarf back on and brushed the dust into the fireplace to mingle unnoticed with the ashes.

The day was now moving on. I retired to the kitchen for something to eat. We grew our own vegetables when in season for the stew as it saved money. Ma was in the garden picking an assortment for tonight's feast. She washed them in the bucket outside and gave me a carrot to eat. I took it, and ate it outside whilst refreshing the water bucket.

The specialty of the evening was to be a mixture of potatoes, carrots, and parsnips, seasoned with a few dried herbs—as always. Occasionally if a chicken was getting old, or was injured, it would get its neck wrung, stripped and gutted, and that would get chucked in as well. I hated the stuff. I remembered the sweet sticky taste of the bun that I had secretly eaten that morning, and it made me hate the stew even more, and hate my parents even more than that. I had seen them take coin after coin each evening from the guests. Alright, I was not that daft to think that the bread and ale was free, but they must have made a tidy sum each evening. What were they doing with it? I sure didn't see any of it. It would not have been too much to ask to have few new clothes each year, or a different meal on the table like normal folk had, would it?

I had to find more coins. The need was desperately brewing inside me. My eyes were getting twitchy. I was constantly studying the floor in the hope of a find, and despite knowing that I would find nothing yet, I still looked.

We all returned back to the kitchen.

"Ma?" I asked tentatively. "What do you do with all the money that you make?" I kept my head down in a humble position whilst I asked her. Curiously she did not flinch from her task her hand.

She just calmly replied, "And what money would that be, Sam?" Only now did she cast her eyes in my direction.

I plucked up a little courage, and raised my head. "Well…I see you take money from our guests each night…and…and…I know that it cost money to give them good food and ale…but…but…I don't see where you put the rest." I took a step backwards in case she swung for me.

"Sam…Sam…" she said softly, and sighed. "Your Pa and I are honest folk. We work all day and all evening just to keep our visitors happy. The baker robs us of our money for this filthy rock hard bread, and the brewers charge us double for a barrel of ale. Just because we aim to serve those who are not wanted, we in turn become unwanted. There ain't nothing left for us to prosper on in our old age." And with that explanation she resumed the cooking preparation. "I am a simple woman with simple needs, your Pa provides all for me that I want." She said this last sentence with a smirk on her face. I knew that she knew different. She hardly ever saw my Pa, and when she did he was mostly either asleep or drunk. "Mind you don't ask your Pa the same question as you have just asked me," she added, "or he will think you ungrateful. We look after you the best that we can." More like the best that they wanted to, I thought to myself.

I was not happy with her weak explanation of where the money went. In fact she had not explained it at all! I had encountered the baker before and knew that he was exploiting our situation, but we had few folk who would deal with us. I might not be able to write my name, but I could count extremely well, and knew the value in money. After all I had learned it by watching the shrewdest of people—my Ma.

Just then there was a knock at the front door of the parlor.

"That'll be Old Tom, he's here early today," said Ma, and she left me in the kitchen whilst she went to open the door for him. "You can brush that floor again in the parlor now the rest of that dust from before has settled, and Old Tom's here now to open and close the door for you," she called from the other room. Dust settled? I thought. Did she know what I had been up to or was it just a figure of speech?

Chapter 5

Old Tom

Old Tom was a curious character. He hardly ever spoke accept for the odd greeting to the guests and a "Thank you, sir" every now and then. I think him to be around 50 years old, but I am unsure. His appearance made him look more like 70. His coat was of the roughest weave. It must have been a dark blue color when new, but it had seen so much sun and dirt that all the color had gone, expect for a small triangle of cloth that peeped over the head of one of the large deep pockets where the stitching had broken. He never took it off whilst serving, even on the hottest of mid summer days. His shoes looked as thought they had belonged to a gentleman once upon a time. But now they where held together with odd laces and had more than one hole in the sole of each. He never wore a hat, but kept his long grey hair tied back with a black ribbon. His face was often unshaven, but not entirely unkempt. He walked permanently with a stoop, though without the aid of a stick, and his eyes were constantly twitching and looking everywhere except where you thought they should.

This evening Tom took his place by the door as usual. I was still in a sore mood for not having found any more coins, and my annoyance was etched upon my face. Pa was back from his merry jaunt with more ale and was busily watering down three of the four barrels. He hadn't brought any extra rum back with him today, except on his breath, as none had been consumed from our stock the evening before. Ma was flurrying around the kitchen, and I was leaning on the wall near the parlor to kitchen door. From here I could see everyone in our inn.

As I watched, waiting for the first visitors to arrive, Old Tom sat like a quiet mouse. He kept looking all around, even though there was no one in the parlor yet. Every now and then he would lift his hand to the latch, but then bring it back down to his lap. I would have thought it a strange action had it been from anyone else, but Old Tom was just a simple idiot with little needs. Then his twitching gaze caught mine, and he smiled at me. I looked away, half in shock of being caught watching him, and half in shy curiosity at his smile. Maybe I would keep my own eye on him later. The sun was now low on the horizon.

Suddenly Old Tom called, "Guests...guests," and sprang to his feet and opened the door. The first of the visitors entered, nearly knocking Tom over in their rush to get in. It was all hands to the deck, The Four Keys was off on another night's voyage.

Within minutes the room had almost filled. Ma always left it until it was nearly full before she made her overpowering entrance.

"Gentlemen, gentlemen, please some quiet..." she paused long enough for them to hush and turn and face her. "Ale all round?" she cried, raising her arms to encourage the crowds reply.

"Aye," came back the chorused answer, and so the routine started again. Ma glided around firstly with the jugs of the better ale, and I followed with the tankards. The guests grabbed and groped her playfully as she waltzed by, and she teased them by dropping their money in to the front of her blouse where she had placed a small purse between her bosoms. It amazed me how she kept control of it all. I will give her that point. She ran the inn with an iron rod. What she said went, and no one dared answer her. She was a larger-than-life character, but still for all intents and purposes a single woman running an illegal inn night after night. She couldn't count on my Pa, as he was always too busy in the kitchen, watering himself and the ale. But the evenings ran as smooth as they could, considering the type of personages about the room.

The Four Keys was the only inn within walking distance from the nearby harbor so our clientele was a little unsavory to say the least. Ale was not what they really needed; they all really needed a good wash. But as ale was what they wanted, that is what they got. Many were sailors that came, or should I really say small time pirates, most already drunk from the ship's rum, seeking a change of scenery with a foot and a sleep on firm ground instead of the rolling sea. Our local village was about an hour or so to walk to back in land, and although it was nearer to the harbor, because it offered no drinking places, the visitors came to us instead. The villagers were aware of our inn and the reputation of the guests that frequented it, but as long as we kept them and their drunken ways away from their little homes and their little lives, they left us in peace.

The evening wore on and the stew had all been served. The guests ate it with vigor and swore it was the best they had tasted. Which pleased my Ma. Truth was it was probably the same as they had been eating on board, but a different face serving it made it seem nicer. Two of the guests who sat near Old Tom took pity upon him and passed him their bread. He thanked them most kindly and then rose and went outside to eat it. I made my move and bolted for the kitchen door and ran as fast as I could through the back yard and around the side of the parlor. I kept close to the wall with my back and edged towards the front. Carefully peeping around the corner, I could see Old Tom. He was muttering something and breaking the bread in his hand into smaller pieces. Then with one almighty throw he threw it all away. A strange thing to do for a tramp who is supposedly always hungry! Muttering again he turned to enter the inn. But he stopped, and looked in my direction. I quickly bobbed back and made a run for it back around the inn. By the time I had got back inside, Old Tom was back in his usual place near the door, his hands shaking as usual, and his eyes twitching. He didn't look in my direction, perhaps he had not noticed I had been missing, but I was sure that he must have heard me stumble when running back, he wasn't deaf.

Normally around this time of evening I would make my excuses to Ma and retire to sleep in the kitchen. All the tankards, stew and ale, would have been dished out so there would be little need for me. But my need for coins was holding me awake. Old Tom was always one of the last to go; perhaps he collected them from the floor, and that was why I couldn't find any. I could not believe that this bunch of fools that had come to visit us this evening would have such a tight grasp of their money all night as not to drop even one penny. I slumped to the floor near the parlor and pretended to sleep. I pulled my headscarf lower so that it looked like it covered my eyes, but left myself enough room to still be able to see.

Pa was fast asleep on the kitchen floor, I could hear him snoring, and Ma was seated at one of the tables having a good laugh with some of the guests. Old Tom though had moved. Where was he? At first I could not tell, but then I spotted his feet shuffling around the back of one of the other tables. With his hunched position he was no higher than the seated men, so moved unnoticed around the room. Each table was involved heavily in their own discussions and too drunk to feel the old man push by. I watched him move around for about ten minutes and then he returned to his seat by the door. He had kept away from the dark corners and just seemed to concentrate on the main central floor area. Ten minutes later he stood up and wandered again. His stoop seemed a little lower this time, but it was hard to tell from my low sitting position. I would need to get a higher viewpoint to see what he was doing. I crawled out of the parlor and back into the kitchen and across to the back door. At this time of night I knew that it would now be locked so carefully and quietly climbed out of the window like I had done so many times before.

I crept around the outside of the inn until I was underneath the parlor window that opened onto the side. The heat from so many men chatting and pushing around had warmed the air in the parlor, so someone had opened one of the shutters wide. I placed my fingertips onto the window ledge and slowly raised myself up until my eyes could see into the brightness. My shadow was cast across the path outside from the many burning candles that lit the room. This window did not directly over look a table so I was not going to be immediately spotted by any of the guests that sat nearby. If by chance I was, I had the excuse ready that I thought I had heard a fox in with the chickens and had gone out to check. I looked around the room. Old Tom was not by the door. After a moment or two I spotted him bending behind one of the drunken sailors. This sailor sat on a bench with both his elbows pressed onto the table and his head resting in his hands as he listened intently to what was being said by one of his mates. Tom seemed to brush against his coat and then moved on. His next stop was of a similar positioned and dressed man. He too sat leaning over the table, but this time he was the storyteller and waved his arms in the air to exaggerate the size of what ever it was he was lying about. Tom brushed against his coat, which hung down over the bench, and away he went. Then it dawned on me. Old Tom was a thief. A thief robbing a thief. I dared not watch anymore and crept back to the kitchen window and climbed in. I lay on my sacks wide-awake puzzled by what I had just seen. Why the crafty old devil. No wonder he didn't eat the bread, he no doubt bought himself fresh every day from his pickings. But what a disguise. A poor old tramp seeks company and warmth in the inn every night. A servant for a few morsels of food. He wasn't making do with the worst; he was creaming off the best.

I fell asleep.

For the next few evenings, I pretended the same game. I played at lying asleep in the inn and then crept out through the window at the appropriate moment. All the time I was watching Old Tom. He did the same thing night after night. Hobbling around to check out his prey first, then returning later for the kill. He never robbed more than two or three people, and what ever it was he took it was only small. He would make his selection and then go outside, wrapping each item in a small piece of cloth so that they didn't bang together or get damaged, and hide the object deep in one of his many coat pockets. At the end of the evening he did not search the floor as I had suspected but just scampered on home to his hut in the woods.

His activities had so fascinated me that I had at least for a few days, clean forgotten about my own search for money.

Chapter 6
Training

I stewed about, and chewed over the idea of Old Tom robbing the robbers for over a week in my mind.

Tonight it all went to his plan as usual. Around the room he bobbed. In and out of the inn he popped. I stood watching from my viewpoint outside the inn, and then just as I was about to retreat back inside—he caught me.

For just one moment I had let my guard down and my thoughts wander, and the next thing I knew someone had grabbed me from the back. One hand was over my mouth, and the other arm wrapped around my chest trapping my arms. He pulled me backward away from the window into the back yard. I stumbled and slipped all the time trying to gain a foothold. I wanted to call out but his grip was so strong and sudden that it knocked my breath away.

When he had dragged me around the corner, he let me go. Completely free. And he stood a good arm's length away.

"Well," he said quietly, "what are you going to do? Run? Shout? I think not!... You are too wise for that." He waited for an answer.

I stood there stunned. Gaining my breath again, and replied, "What did you think you were doing just then? You could have made my heart stop? What are you doing around here? You were at the front a moment ago." I bombarded him with a range of quickly fired questions, not giving him the time to answer one before I got onto the next, waving and pointing with my hands in exaggerated gestures as I spoke.

"Well..." he said again, quietly, "I thought it best that I caught you before someone else did."

"What do you mean?" I asked.

"Well, if I know that you have been outside that window all week, then I am pretty sure that other regulars do as well, and they might not look upon it too kindly, a sort of spying on them they will think, and besides I have my own skin to think about." He took a deep breath and continued, "If you get caught, you might blab about me, as I know you have been watching me." He stood there defiantly, looking remarkably straight-backed; not his usual stooped position at all.

"Er…no, no, I wouldn't do that," I insisted.

"How do I know?" he inquired.

"Well…" said I, my brain running just a fraction ahead of my mouth. "I want in on your deal." I thought quickly, changing the reply to his original question. He had had a point. I might have told, but then again I might not have.

"Oh, I see." He breathed heavily and slowly, in and out, for a moment. "And what deal do you think that is?" he asked.

"I know what you have been up to," I said proudly and quite loudly. I straightened myself up tall, to look important. "I know that you have been robbing our guests of their money."

"Those are strong words for some one with no proof but the eye of a youth. Who do you think will believe you when you speak out? You have no age to offer any authority around here. You don't even stand up to your Ma and Pa, so what makes you think that you will be listened to by a bunch of robbers, thieves and pirates?"

Again he had a good point. Most of the guests had never even heard me utter one word, so if I suddenly broke out into a long pompous speech about the rights and wrongs of folk in the inn, I would certainly get laughed at. I bowed to his judgement, and returned to my rather sheepish stance. It was better I said nothing. Still I wanted in on the deal.

"I hate it here, I want to leave, and this way…your way…is the only way I can get enough money to get out of here." There I had confessed to Old Tom my reasons.

"Hey, Sam, believe me, life is no better out there," he pointed to the country, "or there," he pointed to the sea. "I have seen it from all sides. I was a farm laborer until I was fourteen. Fed up with the way I was getting treated I ran away to sea. I joined the Royal English Navy and after ten years I found myself on one of the fleet of ships commanded by Captain Avery. He was a good sailor, but let the tease of vast fortune lead him astray. I stayed with him when he swapped sides and went to work for the Spanish as a privateer. I have seen what money and wealth can do to a man. He became more and more obsessed with the treasure and turned into bad man. Still, more fool me I kept with him as this life was all that I knew now. I was at sea for a total of more than 20 years in all. It's a hard life. The poor food and the cat of nine tails bent my body to this what I am today. With the turn of the century, I made my mind up to get back onto firm ground."

I was completely over whelmed with what Old Tom was telling me. There was I just thinking he had crawled out of the woods. The man had seen more action than most of the half-bit pirates that visited our inn. I continued to listen entranced by what he was saying.

"So Sam, I says to myself, what am I going to do now. I had a little wealth left. I had been filthy rich at one stage, but just like those poor men in the inn, all I had the sense to do with my money was gamble and drink ale. It doesn't last forever, and it doesn't mean as much as a safe roof over your head. Now I am penniless, and borrow a few things from the guests to save me from starvation. I know that I will get caught one day, and probably meet my death at the same time."

Old Tom turned to go back in.

"But Tom," I pleaded, "doesn't everyone deserve the chance to make their own minds up about their future. Please don't let me live this life forever. It may suit you now; you have seen everything, but I have not lived yet, and until I have I need to feel more, to see more, to become more. The only way a man can live out his dreams in this world is to have the money to buy them. Please help me, Tom." I was close to tears. My master plan to escape was starting to crumble. But I must have touched a nerve with Tom; he turned back to me.

"Aye, you are right, Sam. I can speak from experience, but you can't. I can tell you things with wisdom, having been there and done it, but you have not. Until you try it for yourself, you will never know, and never listen to anyone who has." He seemed tender and caring when he spoke and patted me gently on the shoulder. "Come on, let's get back in before we are both missed."

We quickly departed the side of the inn. Old Tom went back in through the front, and I climbed back in through the window. Once back in the parlor, Old Tom regained his position by the front door and I by the internal kitchen door. He looked over to me and made a friendly gesture with his hand. Then he pointed to his eyes and then to the room. He was indicating for me to watch the guests. So this was his first move then. He studied them all from where he was to see who would be the easiest to pick. I nodded my head slowly to acknowledge his sign and watched.

For the first time since I had been allowed to serve in the parlor, I actually watched, and looked carefully at the guests. Tonight's flock of misfits consisted of approximately 45 sailors, all pirates no doubt. Most of this lot had also been in the night before so faces started to look familiar. There were three of the dark corners occupied by about ten of them, the fourth corner contained a solitary figure, whom everyone seemed to keep their distance from. The remaining sailors were scattered amongst the middle tables. Some were playing gambling games, and one had a small flute-like instrument and was playing tunes. Several joined in with singing, and the rest were just sober enough to prop themselves up at the tables. The room was filling with smoke from their pipes and two windows had been opened.

They were mainly dressed in fashionable clothes of the time, although they were rather dirty and tattered. Some had striped tops like the navy wore, and a couple had expensive-looking silk shirts on. All no doubt been taken without the owner's permission. Most men had headscarves of assorted colors, tied at the back of their heads in a similar fashion to my own. Around their waists they wore thick leather belts, and under their jackets hung a variety of slings containing several pistols, no doubt loaded, and an assortment of daggers. None carried cutlasses except the few seated in the dark corners, who I therefore assumed to be of a higher ranking on the ship. Maybe even captains.

The men in the dark corners were a little harder to see. They kept their heads down and close together, occasionally looking up when the noise of the room altered. Plotting their next raids, I thought, as small maps were often brought out, unfurled, studied intently and then hidden again amongst their clothing. The only man who did not seem to be interested was the person who sat on his own. He was dressed mainly in black and wore a tri-cornered hat with a red ribbon. Much more of him I could not see as it was too dark. The other men seemed to know who he was, and didn't bother him. Ma still served him just the same so I must have delivered his tankard to his table. But until now I must say that I had never looked anyone in the face.

Old Tom didn't arise from his post again that night, and I got very tired and took my leave to go to bed. I glanced at Tom, who could see that I was tired. He nodded and tipped his head in the direction of the kitchen to bid me goodnight.

For the next few nights the same group visited us. Their ship must have been in port for quite a while. Normally, although we did get repeat business, we could go months before the same faces came back. The same sailors played games, and the same sailors sat in the corners. The solitary man did come back as well although I never saw him come in, but on most of the nights left earlier than the others. Tom seemed a little wary of this bunch. There was only so many times that he could rob them, so he remained quiet and extremely unobtrusive until the next fresh lot came in. Every now and then he managed to say an odd word to me. Mainly "wait" or "times not right" or "keep watching." I studied our guests so hard that I could even tell if they had just brushed their beards. I knew if their clothes had lost buttons. I knew if their daggers had been used, and I could spot a loaded pistol from across the room. When I delivered the tankards and bowls, I now looked them straight in the eye and acknowledged them. I started to chat a little, mainly greetings or compliments, to which to my surprise they always politely responded.

Ma, I could tell was getting a little concerned over my actions. She started to watch me like a hawk when I was serving, and for once would be a little quieter herself. But the guests liked it, so she let it be for the moment. Every now and then I could hear her grumbling in the kitchen to Pa.

"That Sam is getting a little familiar with the guests…Pa…Pa…look at me when I talk…Sam is getting a bit too friendly…too confident all of a sudden…the other one went like this…remember…Pa?" Pa was obviously too drunk to take her on, so she hit him over the head with the ladle.

"What in heavens name did you do that for, woman?" he growled, rubbing his head.

"Just you answer me when I talk to you," she scowled back.

"Yes, yes, alright, yes Sam is getting confident, but it is about time." He continued to rub his head, and drink ale at the same time, spilling most of it down his shirtfront.

"I don't like it, Jacob…just you wait and see…I don't like it…a child needs to be kept in its place…not to get familiar with the guests…the other one got too cocky…started to ask too many questions…and look…look what he did…went and left us with this one." This one, I presumed was me, and the other one I presumed was my brother.

"It's just the age," replied my Pa. "I'll sort it all out tomorrow, have words and things," and that was his final response. I knew that he would have forgotten by the morning, it was just the ale talking at the moment. His body and mind were so pickled that he was unable to remember anything except how to get to the brewery. I had my doubts though, I think the donkey had more sense. But my Ma would not have forgotten. I needed to get out early the next morning before she arose.

Chapter 7
The Waiting Game

Luckily, the next day, Ma had left the bakery money on the table. She often did this if she wanted a lie in. So after I had boiled the eggs, I quickly grabbed it, and made my escape. I would wash the dishes and do the other chores when I got back. Ma wouldn't like it, but as long as they were done before the guests arrived, she really didn't have too much to complain about.

I stomped all the way to the bakery and got the bread as usual. I know it had only been a few days of watching, but I was eager to do something. I took the bread off the baker without saying a word. I just handed the money over, grabbed the bundle, and left. He stood at the door looking a little puzzled as normally I was very polite and always thanked him. He shrugged his shoulders as though to say "just one of those things," turned and went back in before I had walked ten yards away.

I started to stomp all the way home as well.

Then suddenly I could hear my name being called. Very quietly, like a whispered shout. I looked around but couldn't see anyone. It was a little eerie. There, I heard it again. "Sam," someone breathed out loudly.

"Who is it?" I cried back.

"Over here, Sam, behind the old tree."

I turned to my right. The old tree, as it was known, was said to have stood for 400 years. It had been here long before the village, and was looking very haggard and weathered, but still it stood. Just behind it I caught a glimpse of a jacket.

I know that jacket, I thought to myself and called out, "Tom, is that you?"

"Shhhhh," came back the reply. "Don't let the whole village know I am here, it's none of their business." And he scampered off in the direction of his wood, beckoning for me to follow. I jumped over the low stone wall that bordered the road and ran across the field in the direction of the old tree, and then onwards towards the wood.

When I reached the wood, I stopped. I had never been in here before. I had only ever preferred to venture in wide-open spaces, like on the cliff top.

"Sam, over here," Tom called. The voice came from my right, so I plucked up courage and headed into the woods in a right-ish type of direction. It was very dark in there. The trees grew so densely that next to no light was let through. There was little grass on the floor, just mainly broken twigs and other bits that had fallen from the trees. Many years' layers of rotting leaves made it soft underfoot, and apart from the odd snap of a fallen branch under foot, there was no sound. After only a short distance I came across an old stone cottage, it was very small, but complete. This must be were Tom lived. I knocked on the door and he told me to enter.

Inside there was just one room, and it was very dark too. A small candle burned, casting strange shadows across the floor and walls, highlighting some of the strange objects he had stood on several shelves. There were what appeared to be many sailing souvenirs. Rolls of ropes, folded sheets, which looked like a thick material like the sails of ships were made from. Some driftwood. Some crockery, cutlery and other cooking implements. A few strangely decorated tins stood in a neat row on one shelf, some with pictures upon them, and others decorated with patterns all that I had never seen the like of before. There were also some unusual twisted metal ornaments, and the rest of his furniture consisted of one table, one chair, one stool, one bed and a large pot hanging above the fire to cook in, similar to Ma's but not as large.

"What did you want me for, Tom?" I asked.

"I have been watching you this last few days. You have been looking good and hard, and noticing a lot, haven't you?"

"Yes," I replied, for I had surely seen many things about our guests within the last few days that I had never noticed within the last four years.

"But," Tom paused, and his voice sounded more seriously, "you are not ready to do anything yet."

He knew that I was eager and wanted to move on, so when he said this I was greatly disappointed, and it was apparent upon my face, and in the posture of my body.

"Don't be so down, Sam, your time will come, and you will get all that you want and need. Just let Old Tom take you through it slowly. I have been doing this for many a year now, and know the ropes backwards. To be good at it you have to learn patience. It's like a game you see, the longer you wait, the better the game is when you get to play it." He stopped talking and took a bottle from under the table and had a good long drink. Rum, I presumed from the shape of its container. He was obviously getting paid well from his thieving to afford rum, and as a matter of fact he didn't look very thin either, so was obviously eating well too!

"This is what you need to do, Sam." He leaned in towards me, although who was going to hear us in the middle of the woods I didn't know. "Carry on the way that you have been, as what you have learned has been good. Carry on making pleasant conversation with the guests, as this will make them think you are of nice sorts. But," at this he sat upright again, well as upright as he could, "start to listen to what they say. As you make pleasantries with one table, have an ear on the next. You can't hear what is going on when you are stood near the kitchen door, you need to be on the floor, amongst it all. The pirates especially like to brag about what treasure they have...shall we say...come across. I know I was one of them." He took another swig from his bottle and wiped his mouth across his jacket sleeve, just like what our guests did. "I didn't get to stay alive all this time by just watching...which is not that easy, mind you, with my eyes..." He pointed to his twitching eyes. "Good for watching two things at once," he said with a laugh. "You have to listen now. So go home quickly, and say nothing. Carry on as usual and come back to me when I give you the signal and we will take this further."

I rose to leave. "Oh, what will the signal be?" I asked.

"You will know when you see it," he replied.

I left the cottage and swiftly made my way out of the wood. Stopping and looking around before my final exit to make sure that there was no one to see me.

When I arrived home, Ma was up and preparing vegetables. She was just about to chastise me when I gave her the bread and said, "Hello Ma, I didn't want to wake you by washing and brushing so I went for the bread first."

She grunted at me, but this explanation of my disappearance seemed to do. I quickly carried on with my chores with a new enthusiasm. My final plan to get away from here was taking a long time, but it was slowly all falling into place.

For the next week I followed Tom's advice and started to watch and listen. At first it was a little hard, for when I was greeting or replying to one visitor, I felt that I was missing what was being said on the other table behind me. But after a while I learned that not only would the pirates tell a good tale, but also they told it several times over the same night, each time it getting a little more exaggerated than before. So what started off as a find of one chest of coins, had developed into a find of ten chests of coins by the end of the evening. Old Tom kept on turning up as usual, opening and closing the door, and making a few journeys around the room, the number of journeys depending upon whether we had repeat business at the inn, and the number of guests in the room. Obviously, the fewer the guests the lesser the journeys. Ma continued to watch me as well, but she still couldn't put her finger on what I was up to. I gave her no reason to cross me, and was in fact turning into a miniature version of her. I chatted more freely with guests and served some of the ale when their tankards had run dry. I started to feel more confident with myself, thanks to Old Tom and the plan. The guests were just ordinary men that had strayed onto a bad path of life. Until this time, I had felt very sorrowful, but now I felt that I was starting to come into my own and hold my head a little higher.

I heard some wonderful tales, and some very heart-stopping, stomach-churning tales. The guests would thrive off giving every detail of how they battled a ship, and killed every man by pistols and blades. The horrible tales I would walk away from. But the tales of finding treasure—I was entranced with. Many a time I spilt the ale when topping up for being too busy listening to their amazing stories. But for all I knew stories and tales they may have only been. All the words could have been made up. After three weeks on intense listening, I had traveled the seven seas with them. I had been to many an exotic port and knew of many strange customs and religions.

My patience in this waiting game was now starting to get frayed. My actions started to slow, and Old Tom could see that I was starting to sink backwards to my old ways. A further two days passed and then one evening, just as the inn was about to close, for I now stayed up all night instead of going to bed early, he sent the signal. He bid goodnight to my mother as usual, and then turned and to me bowed. He had never, ever done this before to no one. Was he acknowledging my patience? For the Lord only knew how patient I had been, and how much I had watched and listened. So in my head I made plans to go and see him the next day when I was on the way back from the baker's. Tom left, and I went into the kitchen to go to bed. Pa was asleep on the kitchen floor, drank too much ale again no doubt. It was too handy for him to be on watch all evening in the kitchen next to the barrels.

Suddenly Ma stormed in, flinging the door wide open. It slammed hard against the wall and awoke Pa with its sound.

"What do you think you are doing? You spilled more ale tonight than you served. Do you think we are made of money?" She grabbed my shoulder and started to shake me around violently. "And why did Old Tom bow to you? What do you know? I have been watching you. You have been behaving strangely lately. Pa said, 'Oh it's just the age,' but I think there is more to it than that. Well? What have you got to say?" She shook me hard again, all the time digging her fingers deeper into my shoulder. She was really hurting me and I wanted to cry. I was very frightened; she was a very large woman and very strong. "What do you make of this, Jacob? Cat's got Sam's tongue. What is going on? Why do you keep looking at Tom all night? What is he doing? Tell me! Tell me!" She bombarded me with questions, not taking any breath between them, then shook me hard again, and flung me down to the floor. I was just trying to rise when Pa, still lying on the floor, grabbed my leg and pulled me down flat again. He quickly stood up and placed one of his large feet upon my back. I was pressed to the ground unable to move.

"Speak to your Ma when you are spoken to. Have some respect for those that have raised you. Do I have to beat it into you?" He pressed harder and made me cry out loud. "If your Ma thinks that there is something going on, then you had better believe it—there will be! I knew that Old Tom was up to no good. He's been hanging around here too long. Just wait till I see him tomorrow. I'll beat the truth out of him if you don't tell, and if he don't tell, then I'll beat you until you do tell." He removed his foot, and I took a deep breath, but he kicked me in my side causing me to roll over. The pain was intense and it felt like he had broken my ribs.

"There's nothing to tell" I screamed at them. "Leave Old Tom alone, he's not done anything. There's nothing going on." My Pa went to kick me again, but I turned away quickly and rose to my feet. But not quick enough to avoid the large slap my Ma gave me straight across the face.

"You ungrateful little rat," she screeched. "You had better be telling the truth. We don't want to have raised another liar. We don't like liars and can get rid of them just like that." She snapped her fingers in front of my nose as she spoke. "You had better be grateful for what you have got, or else you might just disappear as well." I was very scared. They obviously knew something about my brother that I didn't, and it certainly was not going to be good news. My parents had hit me before, but it had only ever been an odd swipe with the back of their hands—although they had hurt! But my Ma had been concocting the notions in to my Pa's head for a while now that I was up to something. He had brushed the idea aside in the past, but seeing that my Ma was exceptionally seething tonight, he took her side. He was normally more placid, mainly because he was always drunk and incapable, but he did have a fiery temper, which occasionally broke loose when the alcohol was starting to wear off.

I was livid. "It's no wonder he ran away," I yelled. "I can't blame him for not wanting to stop in this house, being accused of something you have not done." I had had a sudden rush of anger, which had made me blurt these words out. I stood frozen to the spot, trying not to predict how they would respond.

"Is that what you think happened?" laughed Ma. "You thought he simply ran away?" She laughed again. "Well I'll tell you what happened, its about time you knew, might give you some thing to think about and get you to change your ways."

"No, don't," said Pa. But it was too late; she was on a roll.

"Your ungrateful little brother got too clever. He tried to blackmail us for something we hadn't done."

"What?" I asked.

"That don't matter," she said, "what does matter is that Pa taught him a lesson, one he won't ever forget. One he won't ever get again no doubt."

"Stop it," interrupted Pa. He looked somewhat ashamed of whatever it was he had done. "There is no need to tell Sam everything."

"And why not? It might teach Sam a lesson. Won't lie to us again when the stories out." She placed her hands defiantly upon her hips, confronting my Pa.

"I said, that's enough. Do you want things to happen again that happened before?" he quietly said. Ma thought for a moment, grunted, and realized that she could open up a whole barrel full of worms if she said anything else. She stormed off in to the bedroom and slammed shut the door behind her.

"Go to bed, Sam," said Pa quietly, and he turned away. I had seen a different side to him that night. Usually he thumped first and asked questions later, but this subject of my brother, obviously bothered him.

Chapter 8
Started

The previous night's activities were still visibly with me the following morning. I was sure that I had a broken rib, and one side of my face was black and blue from where my mother had hit me well and proper. They were both very sore to touch, and made me wince every now and then especially when I stretched my muscles during some of my chores. But the one thing that really puzzled me was my Pa's sudden switch of actions. Normally a loud brash man he always sided with my Ma and beat her point into everyone. But the subject of my brother's disappearance was not open for discussion with him. There wasn't a day that went by that I didn't think of him and his sudden vanishing, and now that my Ma had partially confessed to getting rid of him my thoughts dwelled on him more than usual. So he obviously had not just run away. I must find out more to ease my mind as I was already starting to fear the worst. As Pa had threatened to beat Old Tom when he next saw him, I decided to go and warn him so he could be prepared.

I climbed out the window very carefully and landed with a painful thud on the pile of straw. I had to sit still for a moment, clutching my ribs until the excruciating pain left, and then I made a run for it. I ran as fast as I could in my current physical condition. I had not prepared breakfast today, and Ma had not left any money for the bread. I knew that I would be in for yet another serious beating when I returned, but I must warn Old Tom. At the entrance to the woods, I was weak and in severe pain. My head was dizzy, and I had to lean against the nearest tree. My hearing became muffled and there was a sudden blackness. I passed out.

When I awoke it was dark. But as I opened my eyes further, I could see that I was inside Old Tom's cottage, and he was sat at the side of me holding my hand gently.

"Now then, mate," he said cordially, "have you been fighting. I remember my first fight." He glanced away in to the air as he spoke reliving his memories. "I was a bit younger than you, and he was quite a bit older…beat the daylights out of me…but it learned me to move a lot quicker for the next time now I knew how much it was going to hurt." He laughed quietly. That was the first time I had ever heard him laugh. It was a sort of "ho, ho, ho" type of chuckle. The type that makes you smile when you hear someone doing it. I tried to smile, but it hurt too much, and made me wince again.

"Here you are, sit up a little, and have drink of water. Have you had any breakfast? Awfully early for you to be out getting the bread, isn't it? Ahhhh…" he paused and looked at me thoughtfully, his eyebrows beginning to meet in the middle of his forehead and several frown lines starting to appear. "Did your Pa do this?" I nodded. "Well, if it ain't history repeating itself again," he mumbled quietly, rose and walked away from me. I don't think that I was supposed to have heard his last comment, but I did. He stood with his back to me and looked out of the small window at the side of his cottage. It didn't look out onto anything in particular, just more trees. I slowly shuffled myself into a semi-sitting position and took the mug that was balanced on the nearby stool and sipped the water from inside.

"What do you mean by history?" I asked boldly.

"Nothing to worry yourself about yet, Sam, we need to get you better first, and quickly, so that we can start the next part of training." He turned around again to face me. He seemed more cheery now.

"My Pa says that he is going to beat you up when he next sees you," I told him.

"Is that why you raced all the way over here? Why, I thank you, Sam. You're a good soul. But I am not afraid of your father. He won't face anyone in a fair fight. Sure he's landed a few good lucky punches here and there, and because he's a strong man they have meant something, but I have never seen him carry out a full fight. It is your Ma you should be more scared of. Her tongue has caused a few riots around here. Your Pa just follows orders and sticks up for her. He's just a drunken fool with a big hand." Tom concluded, walked back over to me and took the empty mug from my hand. "Don't you worry about him, just keep out of your Ma's way for a while." He winked reassuringly at me. I felt a little better. Old Tom was obviously very wise and knew the lay of people's characters very well.

"Now," he said, "I have had a quick look at your ribs, and they are not broken. I am sorry for looking without your permission, but when I picked you up in the woods, your shirt hung a little open and I could see the bruising. They will feel much better in a few days."

I was a little embarrassed that he had looked, but his comments were good to hear. He passed me some bread, and helped me back onto my feet. "You had better get back to the inn, quick style, and eat this bread on the way back to give you some strength. If your Ma and Pa has not arisen, and let's hope not, you can pretend that you were outside getting the eggs." I shook his hand in gratitude and made my way out of the cottage. "Oh, just one more thing, Sam, I think it's best that we ignore each other for three days. I will keep myself out the way when your Ma comes near me in the inn and you do the same. It will give them some time to cool down. On Wednesday morning when you next come for the bread, come and see me and I will have worked out something for you to do." He waved as I walked away. At the edge of the woods I checked to make sure that it was all clear and ran as best as I could back to the inn.

Back at the inn I quickly grabbed some eggs from the shed and squeezed back through the window. Although I had been gone for a few hours, luck was on my side and my parents had not arisen. I placed the eggs onto cook, and picked up the broom and started to sweep the kitchen. Ma may not have seemed the type, but she was meticulous about the cleanliness of the rooms, furniture and crockery.

Not long later I could hear them both awake. I could hear a key placed in the lock of the bedroom door and it slowly turned. Pa stumbled out first, for a change, still grasping an empty bottle of rum in his hand, which he had obviously took to bed with him. He groaned and yawned, and flung the bottle out through the empty window. Heading straight for the eggs, he could see that they were not cooked, so he looked around and found a crust of bread left over from the night before. He ate it, creating more crumbs on the floor for me to brush up. Not once did he look at me. After eating the bread, he headed towards the parlor, opened the door, went in, and sat down at one of the tables. He sat with his back to the kitchen door, and didn't move from there until Ma got up.

Ma came into the kitchen and locked the bedroom door behind her. She straightened her skirt, and tucked a stray hair under her cap. Walking straight past me, she headed for the eggs which were now cooked. She silently lifted them out of the boiling water and placed them into a clean bowl. She cursed to herself as she could see that Pa had eaten the last of the bread, and slammed the bowl down onto the table. Pa came back into the kitchen and between them they ate all the eggs and did not offer me a single morsel.

For the rest of the morning, not a word was spoken between the three of us. We all did our own thing. Pa went off to the brewery. Ma slammed the money onto the table for the bread and I went and collected it. I came straight back as we were already running late. Ma snatched it off me and started to cut it into slices. The stew was starting to cook, and the sun was starting to set. Pa came back, unloaded the ale, and I cleaned the parlor.

Then Old Tom arrived. He let himself in through the front door and took his seat at the side ready to start his duties. I looked anxiously at Pa to see if he was going to do anything. But nothing happened. I felt rather uneasy and unsettled with the situation. It was like the calm before a storm, but nobody cracked. After what seemed like hours, Old Tom's voice suddenly broke the air, "guests" he called and the door was opened and shut several times. Ma pushed past me and entered the parlor, and took on a complete switch of personalities. She launched back into her showman style as though nothing in the world had happened.

"Gentlemen," she called out, "ale all round?" And back came the reply "Aye" as usual.

I put on a brave face for the rest of the evening, and Old Tom made sure that he avoided everyone from our family. He didn't even tour the room to see what pickings he could get that night. Ma occasionally glared at him, but he just smiled back. She just could not tell what he was up to and it was eating away at her. But she didn't let the show slip and none of the guests were any of the wiser. I dished out the tankards and served the stew, and made some pleasant conversation, though maybe not as much as usual. Some of the guests noticed that I was hurt and enquired about it, and some did not. I told then that I had had a bad fall when out climbing on the cliff, and this convinced them.

The evening was uneventful, and rolled into the next day. For three days Tom and I avoided each other, much to Ma's annoyance. She was still hoping to catch us at something, you could tell by the way she flashed her eyes at us. Pa after three days of ale and rum had completely forgotten to beat up Tom and was back to his usual drunken self. The conversation had started to flow a little more in the kitchen, although Ma did still give me the odd gentle jab with a piece of cutlery now and then. However, it soon became Wednesday.

My ribs were now feeling much better. As Old Tom had said I had luckily not broken them, just had them badly bruised. My face had started to change color from purple to yellow and all was looking calm again. Ma no longer left the money on the table for the bread, but would give it to me personally, reluctantly, during the morning after I had completed the brushing and washing and so on. I gave her no reason not to trust me and had always returned back on time the previous days.

But today I was going to be a little late, as I was going to see Old Tom on my way back to find out more about getting started with his 'something for me to do.'

Chapter 9

The Code

That Wednesday morning, I went to the baker's as usual. My heart was beating a little faster in anticipation of what Old Tom was going to tell me. I snatched the bread from the baker, and ran away as quickly as I could to get to the wood. Making sure that no one could see me I headed over the field and into the shadows.

Old Tom stood at his cottage door. He was puffing on a pipe, something I had never seen him do before. The smoke rose from it in curious patterns due to several holes and broken bits, and it intermingled with his grey moustache, making it look like it was on fire.

"Ahh, Sam," he said, stopping his pipe sucking to speak. "Over here, tell me if you can follow this." He pointed to a small square that he had drawn on the ground, and inside with broken twigs he had placed more square shaped boxes. "This be a plan of your parlor."

Sure enough when I looked I could see where the front door was, and the chimney. The tables were laid out in exactly the same pattern as Ma had them, and he had even made an imitating attempt of the dark corners by placing darker pieces of fallen rotted branches.

"What we are concerned with is these six main tables. What we are going to do is number them one to six," and he pointed in turn at each and said a number to correspond. Starting with the single table near the back wall this was one, and then onto the other five which were side by side, numbered two to six running left to right as you entered the room. "Our code for the tables will be right hand," and he raised his.

"I don't know what you mean," I said.

"Watch, and you will learn then" he replied.

"Table one will be a clenched fist and your thumb sticking up, like this." He gestured as he talked. "Table two will be thumb and first finger, table three thumb and two fingers and so on, and then finally table six will be tightly clenched fist on its own." Again he gestured. "But you must do this with your hand behind your back, so that I can see, and your Ma can't."

"Why am I to learn this?" I asked, curling and uncurling my fingers in practice.

"Well, it's like this...have I not taught you to be patient?" he asked.

I nodded.

"And have I not taught you to watch and listen?"

I nodded again.

"Well, now we are going to put it into practice. I don't think you are really ready yet but seeing as your Ma is curious, I think it is better we get you out of there before the worst happens. Don't expect it to be tomorrow, it will take at least thirty days to get you a good stack of coins and so on, so that you can get away." He emptied his pipe by banging it on the wall of his cottage, and went inside. I followed.

"But what about you, what will you live on? I know that you need the money as well to feed yourself, as you don't eat any of the bread that gets given to you at the inn, so you must be buying it, or stealing it, from somewhere." I raised an eyebrow, and gave a cheeky grin.

"I do not steal food. I pays my way," he snapped back at me. "Anyway it is not coins that I trade in, it is these." He lifted down one of his strange tins from the shelf, and emptied the contents onto his bed. There I could see small colored stones, red, green, and blue to name a few. They didn't really mean anything to me. "These are rubies, emeralds, sapphires, diamonds, and an odd pearl. I borrow them from the pirates that come in. They can't resist talking about what treasure they find, and very often bring a few bits in to the parlor to gamble with. I takes my opportunity, and I borrow an odd one now and then. They don't miss them...they have loads more back on board. I know what it's like, I have been there and seen it all remember." He started to put the gems back into his tin. "I trade with the baker just like yourself, and he gives me food and other provisions for my stones. He's as dishonest as the guests you get in the inn, but he hides it well, and makes himself a pretty penny out of it as well. Then one day when I have filled the tin, I am going to go to the big town, buy myself a proper house, and live like a Lord and show them all that Old Tom is no fool. Jewelers pay well for these stones as the ladies love them in rings, necklaces and other fancy things. A Lord of a manor I shall be, with lots of money in the bank." He swanked around and waved his coat about as he walked to the shelf and placed the tin back. "So far it has taken me nearly 15 years to come to my senses. At first I didn't realize their value and damn near threw them away, but now I have become wise and drive a hard bargain with the baker. A couple more years I keep telling myself and I am out of here." He gestured at the cottage and beyond into the wood.

"Are they safe up there?" I gestured toward the shelf.

"Oh, aye," he replied. "No one comes near me, think I am a fool, and besides they are frightened of the wild boar in the wood."

"What wild boar?" I asked, feeling a little uneasy myself at the thought of having to get back out.

"Precisely!" He laughed. "Now show me your signs for the tables and then we can work on the next part." I stood, turned my back to him and made the signs. Each time he shouted back a number and acknowledged it with a tap of his foot. "That's very good, now here is what we will do next." He came and sat down on his bed near where I stood, and lowered his voice a little. "We need to get you a good stack of coins so that you can get away, once you are away, you can get a job in another village and that will earn your keep, but until then you need traveling and food money."

I was starting to feel a little nervous about the prospect of leaving. I had never been on my own before, but I was determined to go.

He continued, "I reckon about thirty coins or so will see you through the next couple of months, if you can't find work, after that it's up to you. Also I will need to stock up more on my jewels so that

I can go on my way as well. If your Ma sees you gone, she is bound to come after me to see what I know. She's not as daft as she looks and will soon put it all together." He beckoned for me to come and sit by him. "Now tell me what you have heard when you have been about your business."

I gladly poured out all the tales that I had heard. Some believable, some not so believable. Old Tom listened intently and nodded after each one. He even laughed at a few that contained great sea monsters and other such things. At the end of all my stories, he asked me, "Which of the guests did you hear these tales from?"

I replied, "I heard them from mainly the sailors who sat on the middle tables, those that sat in the dark corners were far more quieter and seemed to be plotting and planning, and as I can't get near them I don't really know what they were saying."

"Aye, that'll be right. They will be the captains, quartermasters, and leaders. Keep themselves to themselves. Didn't get to their positions by being foolish and flaunting their money." He breathed in deeply and raised himself up a little from his hunched position. "But that doesn't matter it's the six main tables that we want. Especially when the inn is full of pirates, as they are the ones that drink the most, fight the most, and remember the least. Now this the next part of the code." He shuffled a little away from me on the bed so that he could turn and face me. "I need jewels, and you need coins, so the code for these will be right hand again, pat your jacket pocket for coins, wriggle all your fingers for jewels. Each time you make a signal I will acknowledge it by tapping my foot on the floor, then you can go on to the next signal. So for example…" he rose from the bed… "this will mean third table, coins." And he stuck out his fingers and then patted his pocket. It all seemed rather simple and quite easy to remember. "I will need you to listen to the tales that they tell and then you need to send a message to me so that I can lift what they have swiftly…and then we are underway." He raised both his hands up into the air in confidence.

I was feeling very happy, and a great big smile etched my face. "But how will you know which pirate to rob, there are usually about six sat at a table?" I asked.

"So this is were the left hand code comes in..." He hesitated before he continued. "I am not going to risk you taking anything...remember I have had far more practice at it...and if by some small chance I get caught...then it will be...." He mimed a knife being drawn across his throat. It made me shiver. For the first time I realized how dangerous this was that I was going to get involved in. He made his way back outside to the drawing of the inn on the ground, and I followed.

"These will be left hand side of table." He pointed to the sides of the tables. "And these will be right hand sides of tables." He again pointed. "This will be signal for left hand side, and this for right." He first stuck out his left little finger, and then left thumb. "You will then need to tell me which guest on that side, and you can simply do this by slow tapping your left leg." And he demonstrated. "After each instruction I will tap my foot to acknowledge. Only make the signals once you have gone back to your place near the kitchen door, and if you think anyone is watching, space them out, I will be waiting, we have all evening. But don't go for more than one stone and one coin in an evening. Choose carefully who you indicate, and listen to many tales before you make your decision. Now go quickly back to the inn, your Ma will be waiting for you." And with that he shoved me away and went back inside.

On the run home, I was slightly confused. Was I to use the code tonight? Would I be able to remember it? If anyone had seen me on that journey back, flicking my fingers, and tapping my leg and so on, they would have thought I was a little mad. Sure enough Ma was waiting when I got back. She cursed at me and clipped me around the head, but I made up a tale about the baker being busy and not being able to serve me straight away, and this seemed to do.

That evening, my stomach was in knots. It churned and it rumbled, and I felt really rather ill. My hands were slightly shaky as I dished out the tankards and served the stew. It was a miracle that I didn't drop any of the ale jugs. Old Tom remained his usual unobtrusive self, opening and shutting the door, greeting each guest cordially as they came in.

Chapter 10
Beginning

Guests poured into the inn. It was going to be a busy night. They usually arrived in groups of five or six; it was rare when someone entered on their own. It seemed that tonight the bulk of the visitors were new faces of pirates that I had not seen before. The room filled quickly and Ma waltzed in with her usual over-painted cheery face on. Pretty soon the ale was flowing and the stew was being gorged. Two of the pirates had brought instruments with them, a fiddle and a drum, and they started to play their songs as soon as they had eaten. Not long after several others started to sing along.

The room was very noisy and the ale was in plenty supply. I was kept very busy ferrying tankards and jugs around. It seemed that these men had bottomless stomachs, and no sooner would I have placed a jug, than they would be calling for more. I was a little tense and could not listen to their tales properly, but after a couple of hours, they slowed down their drinking pace and it gave me chance to wander around. Old Tom stayed by the door all this time and did not move, but I could feel his eyes watching me as I carefully crept around the tables pretending to move dirty dishes whilst I listened.

On top of table one, sat the musicians, playing away what seemed like non-stop music. Nobody else sat here, so to study this table it would be a waste of my time. At tables two and three sat thirteen men. They wore clothes that had been stained by blood. They each carried at least one pistol, strung around their neck on a fancy ribbon, and within easy hand reach. This group all seemed to know each other and banter flew back and forth between these two tables. At table four and five, sat a little squashed group of sixteen men. They didn't seem to know anyone from the other tables, but all being in the same business they easily interacted with the other groups. Their clothes were a little cleaner, and only a few of them had pistols. The rest brandished an array of knifes and daggers tucked into specially cut slits on their belts. Finally at the last table, number six, were seven men. They didn't seem as rowdy as the others but were dressed in a similar fashion and ate and drank just as heartily. All the dark corners were filled as well, with characters a little grander in their stature, dressed a little better, and definitely not looking as rough, and, yes, there was one character that I had seen before and that was the man that always sat alone, dressed in black.

The tales that I wanted to hear now started to emerge. The men filled with drink tried to oust each other's tales by making theirs bigger and grander. One table would brag of capturing a Spanish ship loaded with 20,000 pieces of eight and ten chests of gold, and then the next would top it by saying they had taken 30,000 pieces of eight and twelve chests of gold. Most of the rivalry between the tables was taken in good jest, and laughed off. Occasionally the men from the dark corners would look around at the others and then go back to their secret discussions. Perhaps they were planning to take each other's ships and treasure!

But tales were not what I wanted to hear; I needed to see some hard evidence so that I could signal to Tom. Finally at half an hour before closing, something happened that caught my whole attention.

A man from table three placed a small leather bag upon it, and being obviously totally drunk bet the whole contents of the bag against an opponent from one of the other tables in a game of dice. Being one obsessed with treasure, as all pirates are, he immediately accepted and also placed a small bag upon the table to equal the wager.

"I want to see what I am betting against first of all," he said. One of the other men grabbed both bags and tipped them out upon the table. One contained twenty silver and two gold coins, and other a small selection of the stones that Old Tom collected. I edged nearer the table so that I could watch closer. It was not rare for men to gamble at the inn, so this little crossing did not attract any attention other than from those seated immediately within viewing distance. It was however rare for so much to be bet, normally it was just pennies, or very small trinkets. One piece of eight was equivalent to nearly five shillings, and the gold coins were ducats worth around eight shillings each as well. This amount of money would have kept a families needs attended to for quite a long time.

The other bag of colored gems didn't have any value to me at all, but I heard one of the other pirates' say that was worth at least twenty times more.

"Not a very evenly matched wager, is it?" said the man who had placed the stones. "But I am a man of my word, and I'll take your bet, but you use my dice."

The other pirate nodded in agreement and muttered, "Aye, alright but you to throw first, highest number wins."

The man with the gems threw first. The dice seemed to roll forever, but finally landed with a six and a five. He beamed a big grin, and the others cheered. It was a hard score to beat.

The pirate with the coins took the dice. He blew on them, and whispered something to them that I couldn't hear. He threw. The dice bounced several times down the table as they rolled. One landed a six. The other spun a little but finally settled. The rest of the pirates around the table has stood in silence, but suddenly a large shout echoed out from them ... "six" ...with all the luck of the devil he had thrown a double!

Obviously furious, the man who had lost the gems glared at the other as he scooped up his prize and gloated to his mates in front of him. Suddenly there was a click. The gem man had drawn one of his pistols and pointed it directly at the winning man. His hand shook with anger and the pistol wavered around. The other pirates dove for cover under the tables or lay flat on the floor.

"That was not a fair bet," he scowled, and he cocked the gun even further.

A single shot was heard in the room and the winner dropped both bags onto the table.

"Be it a fair bet or not, you took it knowing what might happen."

A strange voice came from one of the dark corners. It was the man who was always dressed in black and normally kept himself to himself. He remained seated, still in the shadows, but it was clear that he had both arms outstretched, with a pistol in each hand. One obviously had been fired as it smoked a little, but the other had not and was pointed directly at the losing man. "Calm down, and resume your activities in peace or I will make no game of this…I will shoot you, and then you will have no need for jewels or coins." That was his last word, but his pistols remained pointed. His first shot had intentionally missed and instead blown clean through one of the candles on the candelabra that was hung high above in the parlor and provided the light for the main middle section.

The pirates from the floor and under the tables started to take back their seats, and the winning man picked up his bags. The loser reset his pistol and tucked it back inside his holder, and sat down grumbling and drinking ale at the same time. Whoever this mysterious man was, it was obvious no one wanted to cross him. Within one minute everything had resumed to normal and apart from the looks drawn upon two men's faces you would have never known that the dice game had taken place. I did notice one other small thing. The winner had emptied his winnings from both the small bags and placed them in his coat pocket and then conveniently for me placed it over the bench at the side of him. This was it; this was my chance to signal.

I headed swiftly back to the kitchen door, and placed my hands behind my back, but within view of Old Tom. Three, I signaled. Tap, he replied. I signaled coins and jewels. Tap he replied. I signaled again, right hand side and tapped my foot three times. Old Tom acknowledged, but instead of rising straight away to go and get our treasure, he remained seated. I was a little disappointed, as I had expected him to spring into action straight away. I know that he had got the signal as he had clearly been tapping his foot in recognition. But I must respect his decision, and after all it was his life on the line if he got caught. I guess he must have just been letting the atmosphere settle a little more.

Then finally after another ten minutes, he arose and began his wander around the room. He did not go straight to the table, but staggered around a little—as though drunk and bumped into a few of the other guests, apologizing as he went along. Once he had passed them each forgot he had been there. Finally at the right place on the third table he stumbled again and knocked the pirate's coat to the floor.

"Hey, be careful, you drunken tramp," snapped the pirate, and leaned back to pick his coat up. But Old Tom had already grabbed it and passed it slowly back to him.

"My apologies, mate," he said and held his hands out the side to gesture that he meant no harm, and scurried back to his place near the door. I was desperate to know if he had took anything, it didn't look like he had to me, and I consoled myself with the thought that it was better to be careful than to be sorry, and that you can't win them all. But at the same time I so needed it to happen.

Old Tom sat down. I glanced at him disappointedly. But my opinion soon changed as he looked at me with a sly little grin under his long moustache and signaled back to me some of the signs that I had used for him. Obviously, they had a different meaning this time, as I was not about to go and steal. He tapped his pocket, the signal for coins, but to all intents and purposes it looked like he was tapping to the music. Three times he patted it. I took this to mean that he had got three coins, and tapped my foot back to gesture that I had got the message. Well, the sly old dog, he had actually done it. I was on my way.

I gave my excuses to my Ma and retired to bed, but I was so excited that I could not go to sleep straight away. I lay under my covers, listening to the music that was still playing, and thought of seeing towns and cities, and maybe even going to sea. I had never gone any further than the village, Tom's wood, or on top of the cliff. Those fabulous tales that the pirates had told, of far away places, did not seem so fictitious to me now. The vastness of what I had now unleashed was now starting to dawn. It was not just a childish stealing game I was playing, pinching a cake through and open window. I was playing against the experts themselves at a game they had mastered. I was playing with a partner whom although he had been around for years, I didn't really know. I had to trust him, and he in turn me. My life lay in his hands, and he was helping me to escape, and for a reason that I really didn't fully understand.

Chapter 11
More

The next morning I was still buzzing. I was still dreaming, and bore a silly grin on my face as I went about my chores. Luckily, I was the only one arisen so far, and I skipped around the kitchen with the broom humming one of the pirate's tunes. I sped through my work that morning with a vigor that I did not normally possess. Then after waiting for what seemed hours, Ma arose and gave me the money for the baker's. I left the inn skipping and running all the way there and back. I decided that I would not visit Tom that morning as I had already been late back the previous one, and I didn't want my parents to get suspicious. But the need to know what he had got was burning inside me—I would just have to be patient and trust him. Morning turned easily into afternoon, and then in to early evening that day. Without carrying a heavy heart, the day had flown by.

Old Tom arrived again and took his seat. Not long after he hailed the first visitors. Ma waited a little and then walked in and performed as usual. I was a little jittery and twitchy inside, and now and then the silly grin reappeared as I thought about the evening to come, but I performed my tasks smoothly and efficiently and was most friendly to everyone.

We had a full house again. There had been hardly a night lately when we had not. But it was the time of year. Being the summer, it brought the pirates north again as the waters were calmer. During the winter, these guests were few, as they tended to stay in the sunnier climate of places such as the Caribbean. So the colder months was when we often got a change of visitors occupations, and served the thieves and petty criminals.

Due to our location, we caught the passing trade as the pirates traveled up country; it was just a short stop for them. A first chance of the men to get their legs on shore after being at sea for so long. There was nothing that they wanted at the nearby villages, no ale houses and mainly poor folk, so they just called at our inn and usually the following day they were away again unless they were undertaking repairs to their ships. The cove where they always landed was a secluded beach area, offering some protection from the elements because of the cliffs, but also giving a good area to run ashore at low tide. It was located half way between the village and our inn, and Pa had erected a large sign to advertise the fact that we were there to serve the needy. Much of our custom was repeat business, catching it on the way up north and then as a last stop before they sailed out south again to the warmer waters. But there were so many pirates, and often a long gap before them came back, that it was hard to remember faces.

Business resumed that evening. They all ate well, drank well, cursed well, gambled and sang well. Towards the end of the evening I commenced my walk around to spot ideal opportunities. Several had fallen asleep at the tables, so I concentrated on those still gambling as I could see what they actually had to offer. If Old Tom had searched those asleep, he may have found something, but then again he may not. At least with those still awake I could find hard evidence of what they possessed. Sure enough table 5 was playing hard. The dice was rolling fast and the coins being passed around. The men were lively yet very drunk. They still called for ale and this gave me chance to get closer to them. I served them slowly and listened to their conversation. There was one particular man that seemed to be winning more than the others were. He kept putting his winnings into his left coat pocket and then sat upon it. He carried on playing with the coins that he held in his other hand. He seemed the best suited, as he was constantly leaning over the table and therefor leaving a gap between his backside and the coat. The coins could be seen quite clearly through the worn and threadbare material. I made my way back to the kitchen door, and commenced my signals to Old

Tom. He acknowledged and stood up, but didn't move away, he kept glancing around the room but kept his gaze coming back to the man I had indicated. After a couple more looks around, he went after him. I slid down the wall to a seated position upon the floor. I couldn't watch. My heart was beating so loud it was blocking out the noise of the music. Presently Old Tom returned and sat down. Had he done it? I dared not look—I must assume that he had.

For the next 19 nights we continued with this game. There had been four nights when I had not located anyone suitable and although I felt disappointed at this, Old Tom had told me that this would happen sometimes, and should not worry as there was always a double opportunity that cropped up another night.

I had decided to play it safe at home as well, and would not visit Old Tom for my winnings until the day I was set to leave. Then I could just pack up my few meager possessions and grab my money and run for it. I wouldn't have to return back to the inn for anything so didn't risk the chance of getting caught by my parents with a pocket full of money. Also if I could persuade Ma to leave the bread money on the table, I could be away with that as well, and as they would not expect me back straight away I could be far in the opposite direction before they noticed me missing. Just eleven more days to go before it was all to happen. Tom and I had averaged my taking out as one coin per day, and agreed that around thirty coins would be a decent amount to get me underway, and would give a small income to live on until I got another job, this time one that paid me!

Night twenty rolled in and brought with it the usual collection of misshapen men and curious characters. They all sat down, jeered, cheered and cursed. Then slobbered and slopped as they ate the stew and bread, and drank the ale. A few of them even managed to prize a few bottles of rum out of Pa stash, all to be paid for of course in hard currency. I watched them as they ate and wandered what type of background they had come from. I wandered if any of them had been like me, ill kept and longed for escape, and this way of life is what they had chosen - or been forced into. They never talked about their families. They always talked of fights, and battles, and marooning, and far away fabulous places. They talked of tattoos, and women and slitting throats. But of course the main topic of conversation was always the treasure, that they had, were going to get, or had heard about. These men were dreamers, but at least they went out and tried to capture their dreams, and a few made at least part of them reality.

"Sam, Sam, over here, mate." I was awoken from my own day dreaming by some of them calling for more ale. I obligingly went and refilled their jugs and cleaned some of the spillage from the tables.

"Sam, why don't you come and be a pirate with us?" chirped one. This thought had never crossed my mind and I looked at him a little stunned.

"I won't have no child of mine taken away by you lot of filthy beggars," cried back my Ma in reply to the question. "Besides, who will help me wait on you lovely gentlemen, and serve you this fine food and ale?" The pirates laughed loudly. That was more the truth. Not the bit about going off with filthy beggars, but the bit about waiting on them at the inn. If I went, who would do it. My brother had gone. My Pa was always drunk, and my Ma liked to tease and show off to the guests, so that left no one but me to do all the work.

Another pirate called out, "Sam will make a fine sailor. I'll take him on my ship any day. Show him the ropes and like. A fine character—just needs to put a little muscle on." And he pulled up my sleeve and gave my arm a squeeze. I pulled away quickly. "And seems sharp about the head, he'll soon learn the way, and then he can send all his fine treasure back to you, my dear Maggie, and keep you in finery like the lady that you are."

Ma actually seemed to blush for a second, but then gave the man that had spoken last a punch on the shoulder that actually knocked him off his chair. "Lady, that I am, I should have been married to a fine gentleman from up north, if one of your kind hadn't come along and shot him before he got to propose to me." They all laughed, but for once Ma didn't laugh back with them, and she moved onto the next table and joined into their conversation instead.

All night I served. This bunch were certainly going to have to be carried most of the way home tonight, by those that were still capable of standing themselves. I watched and I listened, but I didn't spot any opportunities for Old Tom. I resigned myself to the fact that tonight was just going to be one of them nights, and we would make up for it tomorrow. I was actually very tired as well, and just after midnight went to bed.

As I lay on my pile of sacks, I could still hear the chattering and singing that was taking place in the next room. My sleep drifted in and out for a while, as the slamming of tankards and jugs on table kept startling me from my light slumber. I also heard a few of the guests leave, and them sing and stagger down the lane back to their ships. Finally my eyes closed tight and I was deep in sleep. But not for long!

"Jacob, Jacob," screamed my Ma, and she ran into the kitchen, her face ablaze with fury. "Jacob, Jacob, get up you lazy bastard, get in here quick." She grabbed at his half-asleep body on the kitchen floor, forced him to his feet, and pushed him straight into the parlor.

"I can manage, woman," he howled back her and shook her away.

What on earth was going on? I leapt from my bed, fully awakened by the commotion and went to the window that looked from the kitchen directly in the parlor. It was kept locked from the kitchen side, but there was a small enough gap between the shutters for an eye to peer through. There I could see Old Tom being pushed around by a few of the drunken guests. They were all pointing at him, and waving their knives in his direction. It didn't look very good. I started to panic both for him and myself. All I could think about was what if he told about me? Weak men give in easily in situations of danger to save their own skin. Next thing Ma was shouting and screaming something at all the pirates. They all arose and started to depart the inn. Many of them seemed to be very angry and a few threw some of the tankards, still filled with ale, at the walls in an attempt to vent some of their temper. I was getting very frightened. I had seem many a scuffle in the inn before, many which had even led to blood shed, but they had always been between just a few, and the others had always separated them. This time it seemed the whole room was up in arms.

I ran into the parlor just to see the last of the guests leave. My Pa had Old Tom pinned up against a wall and Ma was bawling at Tom at the top of her voice. "Thief," I heard her cry.

My world collapsed.

Chapter 12

The Fight

Now completely awoken from my sleep my head was filled with many mixed emotions and thoughts, and my blood again pumped loudly around my body.

"Stop it," I cried and foolishly headed towards Pa trying to pull him off Old Tom. "Stop it, you are hurting him."

"He will be more than hurt when I have finished with him," Pa hissed back. I still tried to pull him away, but could not even budge him one inch.

"Sam, get back into the kitchen, this is nothing to do with you," Pa shouted toward me.

"Or is it?" snapped Ma. "You two have been very friendly of lates. I bet you are both in this together. I knew it! I told you ages ago, Jacob, that they were both up to no good. But oh no you wouldn't believe me—put it down to juvenile pranks—I tell you, Jacob—Sam is in this up to here." And she made a slicing action with her hand over her head.

Oh my God, I thought, has he told them? Has he confessed to try and soften the blows and pass the blame onto me? Has he said it was all my idea? I let go of Pa sharpish and moved a safe distance away.

"Sam's nowt to do with this," Old Tom managed to splutter out, as Pa had him pinned with his neck against the wall. Maybe he had not told them.

"I don't believe you!" Ma scowled at Old Tom and then at me. Her lips pursed together as though she was going to spit at us. "You two have been planning this for a long time, it's just a pity for you that you got caught tonight. You are nothing but a common thief. Great pirate you may have been in your past life, but since I have know you, you have been nothing but the lowest of the low, a tramp and a homeless waster."

She continued, "And now this is the way that you repay our kindness, our kindness in letting you come into the warmth every night, giving you good food and company, is this the way?" She held out a silver ring. It was obviously one that belonged to a man because of the size of it. But it was rather plain, made of a solid construction and shaped rather square-ish on top. It also looked like it might have contained a jewel of some kind in its past life, but pirates being pirates had probably prized it out. "I confess that we are not without our little sins ourselves here in this humble inn, but thieves we are not. We work hard for our money and people pay us what we are due." She flung the ring under the tables. It landed near me, so I bent, picked it up and put it quietly into my pocket.

"You don't know what you have just thrown away there, do you?" said Tom, still struggling trying to speak. "I was only going to return it to its rightful owner, I was not going to keep it, honest."

"Honest, you are not, a silver ring is just a thing of value to you, a thing that will buy you some comfort, you do not care for other people." Pa spoke and pushed a little harder against Tom's throat, making him choke as he struggled to breathe.

"Let him go," I cried out. "Let him go." And I once again grabbed Pa to try and pull him away.

"I'll deal with you later," he muttered, lifted me clean off the floor, and flung me into the kitchen. Ma instantly locked the door and I was trapped there. But my small diversion had meant that Pa had to let go of Old Tom. As fast as lightning he was out the parlor door and running down the road. For a man of his age and infliction he was as fast as a hare that was being chased. But Pa was soon close on his heels, having suddenly completely sobered up. Ma was not as fast due to her size and hobbled after them, hurling abuse at Tom all the time. I had to get out. I tried the back door, but that was locked too, so I scrambled out of the kitchen window like I had so many times before. My landing was a little awkward as I could not see the ground properly due to the darkness of the night, and I banged my head on the water bucket as I fell. But it didn't slow me and I was soon in pursuit of the others.

Old Tom was heading for the cliff; he must have been hoping that the climb would wear my Pa out, but no such luck. For every step that he took, my Pa took one twice the stride, and by the time they were nearly at the top, Pa had managed to grab him. Ma still struggling, stood leaning on the fence at the bottom, panting and groaning in exhaustion, but still managing to swear and shout.

"Jacob, kill the beggar, he's no more use to us, kill him and throw him off the top. No body will worry about him, be washed out to sea like the other one was, think it was an accident." She puffed and wheezed even more after yelling this out. But what did she mean by the other one? No time to worry over it now I had to help Old Tom, plus I didn't want my secret telling and I needed to know where he had stashed the money.

"Sam, Sam, get back down here, you disobedient fool," Ma called to me as I rushed past.

"No chance," I yelled back at her without even looking. I had to help Tom, but what could I do? I knew that my Ma was unable to climb any further so would not bother me, so I would have to wait and pick the ideal opportune time. I ran behind a small jut of stone that rose out of the cliff. It offered some disguise for me against the moonlight, but Pa and Old Tom were too involved in their fight to notice me.

Punch after punch was thrown, first by one and then by the other. When they landed, they visibly hurt. Pa was a street fighter, he fought rough, and preferred to try and knock his opponent down. Tom was an old pirate; he fought with tactics, probably because when he had been fighting in the past he would have had more than one opponent to deal with at the same time. Pa was tall and heavy. Tom was a lot smaller and leaner, but he stood his ground and dodged and weaved. This was much to Pa's annoyance who had tried to charge him like a bull charging a target, but he just kept leaping out of the way.

"Stand still, you idiot, and fight like a man," called Pa.

"Stand still and fight like a pirate," called back Tom, and he drew a small blade from his belt.

Pa did stand still for one moment, to take account of the new circumstances and to also draw a small blade from the side of his boot. Old Tom obviously had not expected this, but gave a wry smile and started to step sideways in a circular pattern around Pa. I watched, unable to assist either of them. I did not want this to happen.

"No," I yelled out, jumping up from behind my hiding place. "Stop it both of you…please stop it," I pleaded.

"Stay out of this, Sam," called back Tom. "This has nothing to do with you. This is something that has been brewing for a long time. I always knew that if I got caught it would probably lead to my death. I must confess that I wasn't expecting it to happen so soon, but you take chances in life, and this one I lost, even though I was doing an honest thing. That ring is for someone else, Sam, it is for …" But before he could tell me whom, Pa had swung at him with his knife and sliced the top of his left arm open. Blood poured out and this took Tom away from what he was going to say. "This is not street fighting, Jacob, it's fighting on my level," he called and jumped around nimbly nicking Pa's body in a few places with his blade. "Do you know what you are getting into? I ain't no easy push over like the other fellow was." Tom was obviously enjoying teasing Pa with both the knife and his words.

"That was nothing to do with you, Tom, it was an honest accident," Pa said in response.

"That's not what it looked like from where I was. Yes, Jacob, I saw it all, I saw it all happen. You have been here before, only this time I am going to win."

"What happened?" I shouted at them "What happened? Tom? What did you see?"

But neither of them replied. They continued to swipe at each other with the blades, putting cuts on each other's bodies like for like. Pa was obviously slightly better at this than Tom had anticipated and was giving him a good run for his money. They continued to move around, each on opposite sides of an invisible drawn circle. The blades would clash, and then be pushed away. Their sweat and eyes glistened and twinkled in the moon light that bathed them enough to give them light to fight. Pa was tiring, he looked to the ground for a second of rest, and Tom struck. Hard into his side his blade penetrated, and the blood poured out, a deep deep maroon. In shock Pa dropped his knife and fell to his knees, clutching his wound. Tom went for the strike again to finish him off like a snake with his useless prey. I stood there mouth open, I didn't know what to do. I never thought that Old Tom would be like this with my Pa, but obviously there was an old grudge to be repaid somewhere from a long time ago, and now he had his chance; he wasn't going to waste it. And yet I felt for my Pa. I know that I had hated him these last years since my brother had gone, but he and Ma were the only family I had left.

But the fight was not over yet. As Old Tom poised his knife above my Pa's back like the blade of Damocles on its final fall for victory, Pa resorted to the street fighting again and knocked Old Tom off his feet. He dropped his knife and rolled towards the cliff edge. Grasping at the ground, he tried to gain a grab hold and stop himself from going over. But it was too late. The momentum of his rolling swung the bulk of his body over the edge and he hung there for a moment by his fingertips. His hands were shaking with the strain of trying to hold on. I ran to the edge and tried to grab his sleeve and help him up, but as I grasped at and touched the cloth, he let go. He stared me straight in the eyes and whispered, "I'm sorry. It's gone." I watched him fall in what seemed like slow motion to the rocks below. I stared at his body that lay broken below on the rocks. His eyes were open and looking towards the sea, the only place he had ever really felt welcome, and his blood ran into the water and mingled and entwined like smoke would in a mist.

"Noooo…" I called out in anger. My hopes of leaving were taking an unlucky path. I rose to my feet, numbed by what had happened and turned slowly to face my Pa. He had managed to drag himself up onto his feet, and was looking at me.

"Jacob, Jacob, wait…" I heard Ma calling from a short distance away. She had managed to get some of her strength back and heaved her way up the cliff. She could see me stood near Pa. But Pa didn't wait; he lunged at me the same as he had lunged at Old Tom. Only this time I wasn't taken off guard and moved to my left. He stumbled, weakened from the battle with Tom and his blood loss. However, it didn't stop him from trying again, and this time he managed to grab my shirt. It tore at the sleeve top as I twisted to get away, beating his hands off me with my fists.

" Jacob, Jacob, leave the little runt to me," Ma called out. But my Pa was not for letting go. Frightened of the beating that I was going to get, or worse, I lashed out with my feet and kicked him hard in the stomach. He let go and bent double. However, this just made him all the more livid, and he lunged at me again. Again I dodged, but instead of coming back for another turn, he was at the cliff's edge and plummeted headfirst over the side. I dared not look. Ma screamed.

"You did that. I saw you. It was your fault. You did it." She pointed an accusing finger at me as she spoke. "I shall get the law. You will hang for this. It was your fault."

"No, he fell," I protested. But she was having none of it.

"You did it. You did it. What am I going to do? I've got to go. Must go." She turned and muttered to herself as she headed slowly back down the cliff. She hadn't even come and looked over. She was assuming that Pa was dead. But what was she going to do? What was I going to do? I certainly was not going to hang around to be accused of murder. It was the word of an adult against that of a child. Old Tom had already warned me that no one would believe things I said due to my age. I picked up the two knives that had been used in the fight, wiped the blood off them on the grass, and then ran as fast as I could down the cliff heading for Tom's cottage. I had to get my money.

Chapter 13

Running

By the time I reached the wood, I was exhausted from the long run. My feet had hardly touched the ground in my haste to get to the cottage. The wind could not have traveled any faster that night. Pain thumped through my head and it felt like it was going to explode. The sky was still very dark as it was still only the early hours of the day. A few stars twinkled and the moon still shone down brightly, watching.

The wood was pitch black. It looked cold and extremely uninviting—but I had to find my money. Bravely I started to wind my way in through the trees. No sounds were to be heard than those made by myself. And each time I made a noise it pierced me with fright. Every twig that I broke with my foot sounded like a pistol shot, and echoed throughout my body and in the loneliness and emptiness of the wood. I had a pretty good idea of where the cottage was, and every now and then there was a small gap in the solid canopy of leaves overhead and a moonbeam would shine through. This gave me some light to see the way but it also cast eerie shadows around. I know that it was only tricks of the light, but they seemed to move in a manlike shape in the corner of my eye, only to disappear every time I looked. Finally I found my destination.

The door to Tom's cottage was never locked, as no one ever visited him. He always had a good supply of candles and lighters just a hand's reach inside as even during the day it could still be dark inside there and everyone needs some light when they are awake. Slowly I lifted the latch, and pushed the door open. It seemed to sigh, and I felt a strange rush of wind leave the house, enough to lift my hair a little and give me a cold shiver. It was like I had freed a trapped soul. As scared as I was, I had to find my money. My Ma slow as she was, in the mood that she had been in, would not have wasted time in reporting my activities. I closed my eyes tight, reached inside very slowly and felt for the candles. My whole arm was shaking so much that when I eventually found them, I knocked them clean off the shelf and onto the floor. Damn it, I thought and went down onto my knees. I started to feel around the dusty ground. There, I felt the same breeze again, this time coming into the house. I shook a little, but muttered to myself that it was only the draft blowing through the chimney and across the room as the door had been opened further. The candles had rolled a little into the room but I managed to feel one and also the lightning tool.

Once lit it gave a warm reassuring glow. I stood up and took a few steps further in. Things looked familiar again in the room. The bed, the furniture, the ropes and odd nick knacks. Turning towards the door to look for the shelves and his treasure tins, I noticed that it had closed. Funny, I was sure that I had left it open, but because of the draft through the cottage it had probably blown itself shut, and in the anticipation of events, I had not heard it. I could see the tins on the shelves. I gathered them all up together and placed them on the bed. I dripped a little candle wax onto the table and stuck the candle upon it so that it would give me free hands whilst I searched. Emptying the first tin, I found a cotton reel and needle. The next tin gave up some buttons and an odd buckle. The third contained nothing, as did the next and the final tin. I knew that this was were he kept his valuables, his own little treasure trove to buy his fine house. Where was it? But more to the point were was my money? Is this what he had meant when he had said that he was sorry it was all gone. Blast the man to hell. He had gone and spent my money! I was furious, like a raging animal I tossed the tins to one side and started to rip the bed covers off. Still nothing. Nothing to be found. It was all gone. I was now shaking with rage not fear.

"Where is it? Where is it?" I called out loudly.

"Right here," came back a reply.

Petrified, I jumped on top of the bed and drew both the bloody knives from the place where I had tucked them in my belt. I held one in each hand and waved them about aimlessly in front of me.

"Who is it? Show yourself," I demanded. Still I continued to wave the knives about, almost blowing out the candle with the breeze from my fevered swinging. "Show yourself."

Another single candle appeared in the far corner of the room, and seemed to float across the air towards me. But as it neared my own candle it was placed upon the table also. I could now see that it was being held by a hand in a black glove. I followed what I thought was the line of an arm and looked toward where I would have expected a face to be, but I could not see clearly, it just looked like one of the black shadows from the woods. I quickly snatched my candle off the table and held it up high, and there stood in front of me was a man of around six feet high, completely dressed in black from head to toe. He wore a three cornered hat on his head that was pulled low at the front hiding his face.

"I know you…" I managed to spluttered out, "you are one of our visitors at the inn. I have seen you before in one of the corner seats." Half-pleased to have recognized whom it was, I still kept my knives waving around. Recognize him was all that I did, as I did not actually know who he was. At least he hadn't turned out to be some sort of ghost or ghoul. But for all I knew he would still kill me, as I had heard that pirates did this in these sort of circumstances.

"My name is Marcus Fleet," he said calmly, removed his hat and bowed his head a little to me. "You have nothing to fear from me. What ever it is that you have done that brings you fleeing here in the dead of night, I can assure you that I will have done something 100 times worse." And he replaced his hat. From the light of the candles, he looked to be around 35 years old, a tall slim and quite a dashing figure. His skin was a deep brown, the sort of brown that you got from being tanned by suns in the Caribbean or Mediterranean. His eyes were of the deepest blue, the color of sea far off shore, and his hair was long and tied back. He was clean-shaven except for a small wispy moustache. He actually looked half-friendly, and had the most mischievous of smiles, and a mouth full of gleaming white teeth, which was unusual for a man of his occupation, which shone out most alarmingly against the blackness of his attire. "I believe you have something of mine, Sam," and he held out his hand.

I lowered my knives, a little, and looked extremely puzzled. What did I have that he wanted? I didn't own very much, only a few clothes, which I had left at the inn and the two knives from the fight. I certainly didn't have any money, as it seemed that Old Tom had very conveniently got rid of that for me.

"The ring, Sam," he snapped, "the ring. Give me the damn ring."

Oh, I had forgotten about that. I put my hand into my pocket and retrieved the ring. So this is whom Old Tom had intended to give it to. "Why should I give this to you?" I asked.

"Because if you don't, then I will show you my true pirate colors and kill you…is that reason enough?" he quipped.

I nodded and passed him the ring quickly.

"Thank you, Sam, you have just saved your little life." He removed one of his gloves placed the ring onto his middle finger of his right hand, and then pulled the glove back on top. He seemed to give a sigh of relief and looked a little more at ease.

"Why did Old Tom have the ring?" I asked. Well, you don't find out if you don't ask, do you? I thought, and I was curious.

"Tom owed me one," Marcus said. "He's been watching out for my ring since I lost it. We knew that it would turn up one day, just a matter of sitting pretty and being patient until it did. Pirates talk a lot. They can't hold their own tongue, unless its been cut out." He chuckled a little. "Like to constantly brag about things they do. I thought he would have found it sooner if he had chose a better spot to watch from, but this is Tom's home county. So…well I agreed to it. Besides, he's not the only one I have on watch duty."

I decided to pry no further, as it seemed from his tone of voice that I was lucky to get this half-explained answer.

"So, I expect, Sam, that you are tired. We can stay here until first light and then be on our way." He pulled up a seat and firmly planted himself down on it.

"But what about my money? Old Tom said he'd keep getting it for me then I could escape."

"A fool and his money is soon parted. Tom was always an old pirate fool. I suppose he told you that he lost all his own money and was reduced to this way of life...well, now he has lost yours as well. It's like water slipping through his fingers. The taste of rum lingers in a man's blood. An addiction that must constantly be fed. A nice enough character he was, but no pirate is honest, and it doesn't take much to send them back down their old path. He may have started out with good intention towards you, but by the end he would have just been using you." He lifted his feet up, crossed them and rested them on the table. Pulling his hat over his eyes, he gestured that I should lie down on the bed.

Well, what could I do? I couldn't run away, as I had no money. Neither could I go back to the inn, or my Ma would have me arrested for murder and I would hang. I was caught between hell and hell's sister. No way to go either way. At least it looked like Marcus Fleet was not going to kill me just yet, so maybe I could think of an escape plan whilst he slept. I huddled into one corner of the bed and pulled the covers up tight against my body. If he did stab me whilst I slept maybe they would offer some protection.

Marcus was right; I was well shattered and fell asleep almost instantly. No sooner had I seemed to shut my eyes though, than a knocking on the door awakened me. My first thought was that the lawmen had come to get me, and as I shook the sleep from my head, I noticed that Marcus had gone. The double crossing rat, he had said that we would be away together at the first light, and now he had gone as well. I cursed to myself as I opened the door. Peeping through a small gap that I had made, I took back some of my curses. It was not the law it was Marcus. He held out a bundle of clothing.

"Put these on quickly," he said, shaking the clothes in my face. I took them inside and closed the door.

"What do I want with these?" I shouted back. "You trying to make me into a girl?" I yelled to Marcus as I unveiled exactly what he had brought me. There in my hands I held a long blue and white dress, a little worn and patchy around the hem, but otherwise rather plain and neat. It was clean, so he had obviously pinched it off someone's washing line over night. Also there was a small grey shawl and some undergarments. "I'm not wearing this," I insisted and threw it back at him through the window.

"Oh, yes you are, my dear," he called back and threw them back in. "Stop pretending to be something that you are not. I know exactly who you are...Samantha Battle."

Chapter 14

No More Pretending

So, that was it! My cover was blown! I had lived my life dressed as a boy, in hand-me-down clothes, and nothing I had ever done had ever given the fact away that I was not male. There were only three people that I knew, who knew of my correct identity—my Ma, my Pa and my brother. I had never had any girl's toys to play with, no dolls or fancy things. I had never worn pretty ribbons in my hair. My complexion and physical size were not typically what I could call girly, more tomboyish in appearance. My parents had successful hidden the fact that I was not a boy for sixteen years, mainly to protect me from the unwelcome advances of the visitors at the inn. Had they known I was really female, I am sure that my virginity would have been forced away from me.

Yes, my name is really Samantha. Samantha Alice Battle, named after some distant aunt or so I am told.

I was stunned and stood there staring at Marcus. How on earth did he know this? No one had ever, ever, called me Samantha. I had been taught to say my name as Sam from being a baby. As I grew up and had started to notice that my brother was different to me, I had been told that it was a game to pretend to be a boy. When I was old enough to know the truth, I still wanted to continue the game for my own safety. Some time when I had felt it right, I would have revealed my true identity. But now it had been taken from me early. I was not ready to live as a woman yet. I wanted to experience the adventure and freedom that only males of my age could. My mood changed into anger, and feeling that I really didn't have any choice now I reluctantly put the dress and other garments on. After a couple of minutes calming myself down in the cottage I stepped out into the woods.

"Well, not bad at all," Marcus said, walking around me and looking me up and down. "You should get away with that until we are far enough from here."

"What do you mean?" I asked.

"Well, I am sure someone will have reported you missing by now, and all the village will be looking for a young boy…not a young female." He gestured with his hand at my attire as he spoke. "Now quickly gather your other belongings and wrap them in a blanket, we must be away from here before it becomes too light." I hurried back inside and rolled my old clothes into one of Tom's blankets, and placed a few other things in as well just in case, like a couple of candles, a cup and a few of his fancy tins. I found a thin piece of rope on the floor and tied it altogether to make it easier to carry.

I quickly scurried after Marcus. It was not easy in the long dress to keep up with him. He seemed to take the most enormous of strides, and did not offer to carry my bundle. Instead of heading back out of the wood, we traveled further in. To his annoyance I was constantly stumbling and tripping, so he grasped one of my arms tightly and dragged me the rest of the way through the wood. The wood was not as deep as it appeared from the other side and within a short time we had come to a clearing.

"We are going to have to travel faster than this," said Marcus, and he grabbed my bundle from me. "Hitch your skirt up, to help you walk easier, there is no one who will see you here." I did as I was told and pulled my skirt up to my waist. I still had my old heavy jackboots on which looked a sight against the lace of the petticoat. Marcus tutted. "We are going to have to get you some new shoes!"

After crossing the clearing we came to a tall stone wall. We both sat down with our back to it. "On the other side of this wall," Marcus began to tell me quietly, "is the road to the next town. Hopefully no one from your nearby village will have passed this way yet. It is still early in the morning and normally only the market traders are passing by at this time. We need some transport, and this is where we are going to get it."

I was a little exhausted from the speed that Marcus had made me travel at, so I was grateful to sit down. I was also very hungry.

"Aren't we going to get something to eat first?" I asked.

"Do you want to be hanging on the end of a rope by the end of the day? Missing one meal won't do you any harm. Shhhhh," he said. "Someone's coming."

From the other side of the wall we could hear the rattle of a little cart and the clopping of hooves on the stony road. Marcus bobbed his head up over the wall so see who it was. "Only a milkmaid," he said, sitting back down. "That is no good to us, we need something bigger."

I sat silently, except for the groaning of my empty stomach as the maid passed.

"Why are you helping me?" I asked.

He looked at me straight in the face with his deep blue eyes and replied, "Well, it's sort of for mutual benefit. I need a companion to travel with so I don't look as suspicious. People can spot a single pirate on land at a hundred yards, and shoot first and ask questions later, but a couple, may look like a father and daughter, or lovers."

I blushed a little.

"Besides what exactly did happen at the inn last night?" he asked.

I proceeded to him about the fight between Old Tom and my Pa, and how my Ma had said that it was my entire fault and that she would get me arrested for murder. "But why were you at the cottage?" I asked

Marcus opened up to me a little more, presumably if we were going to be together for a while I at least deserved a little truth. "Tom had sent word that he had heard of the ring, that is why I have been visiting the inn lately. Last night I had arrived and waited outside. I heard some of the commotion inside and saw that Tom had got the ring, I also saw you pick it up when it had been thrown. Old Tom nearly said what it was, but your parents were not quick enough to pick up on this. It is an old family heirloom, been passed down my family for generations. It should have a precious stone on it, but this has been missing for a long time as well. I need this ring to prove my inheritance. I went to the cottage because I know that you and Tom have been working together, I have been watching you both, and with the seriousness of the situation in the inn I knew that you would turn up there sooner or later to get your money."

I questioned him. "But if you are a pirate, why have you not just taken the ring before now?"

"Pirate I am, and have been for near sixteen years. I have traveled the seas and had many a ship to my command. It has been hard many a time, but I have gained the respect of the most evil men you can imagine. I have slayed many, and killed others unfairly, but when it comes to the holder of the ring…well, let's just say I needed a pickpocket to take it so as not to create a fuss."

"And what about me? Are you going to slay me when you have gained your inheritance?"

"No, my dear, just be patient and stick with me for a while and your new life will be revealed. Now, shhhhhhh, I can hear another cart and horse, let's hope this one is the one for us." He peeped over the wall again and smiled. I guessed this one was ideal. "Now this is what you have to do." He leaned towards me and whispered his plan in my ear. "Don't forget to ask all the questions, and oh take your boots off and leave them here, want to give the right appearance, don't we?"

I was petrified, but did as I was instructed. I removed my boots, climbed over the wall and sat looking all forlorn on the grass verge. I could see the cart coming up the road. It was a medium-sized one, pulled by a good strong-looking horse, and steered by just the one man of around 40 years old. I hated myself for what I was going to do—but I didn't want to die.

"Excuse me, kind sir," I called out. "You going to the next town to trade?" and I pretended that my legs ached and started to rub them slowly, revealing quite a lot of flesh.

"Yes, Miss, got myself a cart of the finest goods. First time I've been up this way," he called back, licking his lips as he looked at me. "Looks like it might be a good visit for me now I've seen you."

"Any chance of a lift, my legs are awful tired," I replied.

"No problem, Miss, just you jump up here." And he patted the seat at the side of him "In fact, I will come and give you a lift." He jumped nimbly down from the cart. I backed away a little and started to ask him more questions.

"Did you hear about the fight on the cliff last night?"

"No, Miss, can't say that I have. It don't surprise me none though if there was one. Probably one of those pirates that I have been told visit here, I have heard that they are the most frightening of men." I was relieved to hear this reply. At least Ma hadn't spread the rumors far, if at all. "Just you jump up here, I will give you a hand." But his hand was not the sort that I wanted; it squeezed my behind a little too much for my liking. "You cant be too careful around here, Miss, I have heard that sometimes those pirates get drunk and wander in the wrong direction back to their ships and end up in these parts."

His hands had now started to stray from my bottom and were slinking their way down to my ankles. He was making me want to heave up. "If I ever sees one, I will protect your honor, Miss, that you can be certain. I am not afraid of those filthy drunken scum."

"Oh, but you should be," Marcus replied, and without hesitation he leapt clean over the wall, drew his sword and thrust it towards the man.

The supposedly fearless tradesman whimpered a little and fumblingly, drew himself a small blade from a leather holder at the side of his belt, which he then very kindly pressed into my back.

"Come any nearer and the girl gets it," he yelled. "I mean it. Don't you come any nearer."

"I am one of those filthy drunken scum that you are not afraid of, yet you hide behind a child. I care not if I take two lives instead of one, it means nothing to me," Marcus smirked.

"Marcus," I called out, starring at him, as the knife was hurting a little.

"Oh alright," he said and huffed, lowering his blade. "What's your name?" he called.

"Jack," replied the man, "Jack Williams." He was shaking; I could feel the blade wobble in my back.

"Well, Jack," said Marcus, "today is your lucky day, you don't need to worry about pirates ever again." He grabbed my arm and pulled me swiftly away, and at the same time drove his sword hard into the man's body. With a final twist of the blade, he fell to the floor dead. I stood there speechless. Marcus wiped his sword on the man's clothing and heaved him over the wall.

"Get in, Sam," he called and climbed into the driver's seat of the cart, as though absolutely nothing had happened.

"What...what...what..." I stuttered and couldn't get my words out, so just kept pointing over the wall and then back to Marcus.

"Don't want to walk to the next town, do you?" He flicked the reins to move the horse, and so I quickly jumped on the back. "He wouldn't have liked it here anyway, too many ruddy pirates robbing you of your goods."

Chapter 15
Traveling

The cart hobbled down the uneven road. Its wheels were oddly sized and it rocked and rolled all over the place. It made me feel quite sick. Marcus was completely unaffected by it, must have been all those years he had spent at sea, learning to keep his balance on the ships. But it was of solid construction and seemed stable enough. The horse pulled good and powerful and therefore there was no reason to slow the pace over the rough ground.

The air was a little chilly that morning as we traveled so I pulled the shawl Marcus had given me tightly over my shoulders. "Where are we going?" I tentatively asked.

"To the next town," he replied. "In fact, let's see what we have for sale here." He leaned over to the back of the cart and pulled away the covering sheet. "Well, that makes a change, a bit of good luck again I would say, at least its something I know about, I was half expecting a cart load of potatoes."

I looked to see what we were carrying. There I could see under the covers, all neatly stacked with a wooden block separating each, a large array of swords and daggers. It made me shiver to think that they had fallen into the hands of a crook like Marcus, and what's more I knew what he would do with these sort of weapons. "It looks like our Jack Williams was looking to do some trade with the soldiers at Castle Market," said Marcus and he threw the cover back over the cart. "Don't want any of those pirates that roam these places to get their hands on these...not yet at least." He winked an eye at me. It made me shiver again.

I decided that there wasn't much for it at the moment other than to go along with his plan. I needed to travel, and he needed a companion. But I had the impression that he was not being entirely honest with me, and there was a little more to it than that.

Looking around the cart, I found a small bundle under the seat. It turned out to be some bread, cheese and a couple of apples. There was also a container full of clean water. I shared the food with Marcus, but his appetite didn't seem to be as large as mine, and I ate the larger share. As he drove the cart, he always looked to be in deep concentration, his mind, I am sure, was planning something one-step ahead from where we were.

The morning rolled by and still there was no sign of the town. "Shouldn't we be there by now, at Castle Market?" I asked.

"Yes, we should, but that's not where we are going. The town's too close to where we have just come from, we need to get a little further," he replied.

"So where are we going then?" I asked again.

"We, my dear Sam, are going to see some old friends of mine at Shepherds Bay....We may stay the night depending on what they have to say...or we may not. I've not decided yet...I'm a free spirit...I come and go as I please....You can't expect me to know everything. I've never slept in the same place for two nights running yet, and I ain't going to change that because you are a soft land lover." He flicked the reins of the horse and made it go a little faster.

I hadn't asked him were we were going to sleep. I only wanted to know which town we were headed to, so that I could plan myself to get away from him.

"How come you knew my name?" I quizzed him.

"Everyone knows your name in the inn, Sam," he said.

"No, I meant how come you knew me as Samantha?" I waited for the reply.

"There is a lot more about you, that I know, that you don't." This reply totally confused me, but it confirmed that he was keeping something from me.

"Like what?" I asked.

"Like things that you don't need to know right now, that's what. Let's pretend Old Tom told me that you were really called

Samantha....There, will that keep you quiet for while?" he snapped at me.

"No it wont," I snapped back. "Tell me what you know or I shall jump off this cart and you can be a pirate on your own again, sure to get arrested as soon as you reach Shepherds Bay. Looks totally suspicious to me a man in black with a dark tan and a cartload of weapons. Obvious that you are planning on causing trouble." I was quite pleased with my little outburst and sat up straight and proud awaiting a reply.

"Alright, alright then," he squirmed as he talked. "You are going to find out soon enough."

I listened intently.

"Your real name ain't Samantha Alice Battle its Samantha Alice..." He hesitated for a moment. "Well what your surname is ain't important, but Maggie and Jacob Battle are not your real parents, and well Daniel ain't your real brother either." He rushed his words out and I was completely shocked. Not only had he just landed me with a complete punch to my parentage, but also he obviously knew about my family in some detail. No one had spoken Daniel's name since the day he had disappeared. He had just been referred to as 'him' or 'your brother.' It was as though it was a sin to say his name.

"I don't believe you," I said, my voice shaking as I spoke.

"Believe me if you want, but I can tell you exactly what happened and how you ended up at the Four Keys, complete with dates, names, towns and places, so that you can go and check it all up if you want."

"Alright then, continue please," I resolved myself to believe what he had to say.

"You was born on February 1st 1700. I was 15 years old at the time so I remember it well. You are the illegitimate child of my cousin Isaac and a maid that served at my father's estate. Jacob Battle was the gardener there. He was a good strong worker but was known for having a few flings himself in those days, result of one was your so-called brother Daniel Jake Battle. Maggie, your Ma, had also been having an affair with Isaac, right ladies man he was, and still is; can't resist anything in a dress, but she was completely distraught at your birth; couldn't have any children of her own you see. Although she always wanted to, she would have never been allowed to marry Isaac due to her lowly background, so he fained his death to get rid of her. And to cut a long story short, Jacob met Maggie. He got paid lots of money to keep his mouth shut and take her away, so they disappeared with both you and Daniel. Therefore everyone was happy, Isaac had got rid of his pain of a mistress and illegitimate child, and Jacob had enough money and an instant family to start with somewhere else." Marcus flicked the reins of the horse again.

Well, what could I say to that? I was completely dumbstruck and sat there with my mouth open. Marcus leaned over and gently closed it for me. He had certainly managed to shut me up this time and I didn't utter a single word the entire length of the rest of the journey. The day wore on and it became early evening.

As we neared the Bay, I could see little houses all packed closely together with little smoking chimneys. There was one main street that ran along on the opposite side to a large harbor and all the houses looked directly to sea. It was really quite busy and people milled all around us, oblivious to the fact that we had arrived. Back home a pirate and a young girl with no shoes on in a cart would have been a strange sight, but here we just blended right in. We trotted the horse down the main street, and pulled into a gap at the side, next to the stone harbor wall. I had never seen so many people together at one time. This was also the first time that I had seen the merchant ships up close too. Men were busy running up and down gangplanks loading and unloading barrels and wooden boxes. The goods that reached the harbor were in turn immediately piled onto carts and taken away, and then more would arrive and be loaded back onto the ships. They were a fine sight. Every man seemed to know his job and got on with it. Their sails were rolled up and men worked in the rigging checking the nets and ropes. Voices shouted out orders and music echoed out from the little houses, some of which I could now see were actually inns and grocery shops. Marcus leapt down from the cart.

"Wait here, I won't be long," he said, "and whatever you do, don't tell anyone what we have." He patted the covered weapons in the back of the cart, straightened his coat, adjusted his hat and headed up the gangplank of the nearest vessel. I watched as he disappeared over the side. A few of the sailors seemed to recognized him and he acknowledged them back as he passed. This ship looked to be crewed by a very rough looking lot. In fact in comparing them to the men on the others ships, they were definitely the worst of the bunch. Although they acted politely to each other, they gave the impression that they were putting on an act and would rather be waving around cutlasses, shouting and cursing. They were obviously being civil due to them being docked in the town. Probably complete opposite of character on sea. They were a very dirty group of men who needed a good wash, a change of clothing and definitely a shave. Most wore at least one knife or cutlass, but no pistols. Several of them kept glancing in my direction and I felt most uneasy. I tried not to look back at them, but they were fascinating me.

After what seemed like ages, but was probably only a few minutes Marcus reappeared. He walked slowly back down the gangplank, but was this time accompanied by another man. This man was dressed in a similar fashion to Marcus, but was smaller and fatter.

"Now then, Marcus, you got a secret that you not been telling us about then?" The man nodded in my direction. "Found your self a pretty little treasure then? Is this why you have been disappearing lately?"

"No," replied Marcus firmly. "And don't you think anything of it, she's a relative and that's all."

"Relative or not, that won't stop many a man." And he started to laugh. His laugh though soon turned into a cough and he clutched his chest. "Got to get myself off this boat soon, or I'll be coughing one time too many, won't be able to walk off and will end up with Davey Jones. Let's have a look at what you got then." Marcus lifted up just one corner of the cover enough to let him see.

"Do we have a deal then?" he asked.

"Aye, come back tonight and I'll have your money. We'll take the horse and cart too. Can't get enough good wood to mend a boat these days, and a horse tastes mighty fine when cooked properly." Marcus shook his hand and indicated for me to get down from the cart. I promptly did so and grabbed my bundle and boots.

"Where are we going now?" I asked as I followed him, weaving through the crowd.

Marcus quietly whispered to me, "I've decided that we will stay the night. It would appear that your Ma has not reported you missing, news is that after you ran last night, she loaded a few heavy bags onto the donkey, set fire to the inn and disappeared herself. Some of the sailors from that boat," he quickly pointed one out, "were at Calland Cove, and because of the beacon she had set going, didn't want to stop for any more trouble so set sail and came around here this morning." So she had taken her profit and scarpered then. Hopefully not in this direction.

Marcus whisked me down the street, until we came near to the end. He shoved me up a side alley and making sure that I could not be seen by anyone instructed me to put my boy's clothes back on. I stood in a deep doorway with Marcus standing guard and changed quickly as requested. My dress was shoved into the blanket bundle and I put my boots back on. I retied my scarf around my head and I was back to being Sam again. Once I was changed, he grabbed my arm and dragged me back onto the street. We stopped outside an inn called the Weathered Man. There was a poster pinned to the outside wall, a wanted for murder poster. I could not read it but could tell this was what it was because of the layout and the drawing of the wanted criminal. I had seen some of these before when I had been to collect the bread from the baker's back home and recognized it as being the same. Funny, the man looked a little like Marcus, but then everyone here did. He ripped it down and threw it to the ground. "Some people deserve better than this when they are innocent…" he added, "no doubt," when he noticed I was watching. We went inside.

The Weathered Man was very much like how The Four Keys had been. It was crowded with people all eating, drinking and merry making. Marcus pushed past the crowd and dragged me to the back as well. No one took any notice of us whatsoever. So this was why I had to get changed—there were no females at all in the inn except for those behind the bar, if you could call them that, and I would have stood out like a sore thumb. Marcus leant over the bar and whispered to one of the women. She turned around, picked a key from a board at the back of the bar and gave it to Marcus. He then pushed me up some stairs and towards a room numbered two at the end of a short dimly lit corridor. He opened the small wooden door and we both stepped inside.

Chapter 16
Sleep

Room number two contained one double bed, a large wardrobe and a single chair. It was situated on the first floor of the inn in the corner of the building. It had two windows on adjacent walls, one that looked over a small alley and the other over the back yard. Both the windows had proper panes of glass in them, and curtains held above them on poles. They opened outwards, and were held locked when closed by small metal hooks. Marcus locked the door behind us with the key, and secured it by way of a large bolt at the top. He walked over to the wardrobe, ever suspicious, and opened it slowly with one hand, and pointed a pistol at it with the other.

"You can't be too careful around here," he said. After seeing that it was clear, he sat down on the chair. I had just stood there on the same spot all the time, clutching my bundle, whilst he inspected the room. "Sit yourself down, lass, on the bed, and make yourself at home while you can," he muttered and dragged his chair over to the alley window and kept peering outside. I was feeling a little tired, and was still in shock from finding out that I wasn't related to anyone I thought I was related to. I flopped myself down on the bed. It was lovely. I had never been on a proper bed before. It had a mattress, and blankets…and sheets…and pillows…and a lovely wrought iron frame. It didn't take long for me to fall fast asleep.

I slept like a log, and for a few good solid hours this time. When I awoke, I didn't want to open my eyes in case it had all been a dream. However, I could feel the soft bed below me and remembered all that had happened. In a matter of one day my whole life had been turned upside down. I was no longer whom I thought I was. My closest friend was still a pirate, but this time not an old retired one, but a young fully active one, and my old home was now a pile of ashes. The only thing that hadn't changed was the fact that I was penniless. I knew that Marcus was now sort of related to me, but still felt that he was hiding some of the truth. Should I stick with him and find out more? Or should I take my own chances and run as soon as I could? Here was I stuck in the middle of it all again. I decided that for the time being I would stick with him, after all he had had plenty chances to get rid of me, relation or not. I was curious what he had planned and had nowhere else to go.

When I did finally open my eyes after all these soul searching thoughts, I found that he was gone again. This was getting to be too much of a habit now. I rolled off the bed and went to the door only to find that he had locked me in. I could tell by looking out of the window that it was sometime in the early hours of the next morning as the sky was still dark to the west but just starting to scrape a little light in on the east. From the noise that was carried up to me in the air, I could tell that the inn downstairs was still just as busy as it was when I had come in the evening before. In fact, it was so noisy that there wasn't a cat in hells chance that I was going to get back to sleep now, so I decided that if Marcus could go out then so could I. After all, I wasn't a prisoner, just a traveling companion!

I looked at the alley below. It was too high up for me to jump down, and there was nothing to climb on. But from the other window I could see a stack of barrels piled up again the wall below me. I quickly knotted one of the sheets to another, and tied the end to the bed head. Slinging the other end out of the window, it left me with just enough material to hang onto until I touched the top barrel with my boots. I had spent a lifetime climbing in and out of windows at The Four Keys, so this one was not going to be a problem.

In the yard, I first hid behind some of the crates there that contained empty bottles, but then moved a little closer to the back door and crouched behind a bale of floor hay. I nearly got caught a couple of times as some of the serving wenches came out to dispose of rubbish, but luckily they always got called back in before they made it to my part of the yard. I had to move before I got found out.

Looking around I saw that the yard had a gate, which was only held shut with a simple lever. Picking my moment, I ran for it, and before I knew it was out in the alley. A drunk or two staggered and passed me by. I pretended to be butch and coughed deeply, hunched my shoulders up, put my hands in my trouser pockets, and moved on. They left me on my own.

I shuffled to the front of the inn. There were several people outside, drinking and singing. By keeping my head down, I managed to needle my way into their group, and joined in with some of the songs. I had heard them many a time back at The Four Keys, so I knew the words well. The group was too drunk to cause any trouble other than the boisterous sort, and too drunk to notice that I was completely sober, but just to add to the act I found an empty tankard, and swung it back and fro' with the rest of them in time to the song.

"Here lad, don't I know you?" said the one who wore a dirty red coat and a round hat.

He may have seen me from The Four Keys, but I was trying to play that bit of my life down now so replied, "No, mate, not unless you saw me earlier getting off one of the ships."

"Aye, that's probably it," he said. "Will you do me a favor and go in and get some more ale? I'd go myself but if I move me legs I will fall over." And he passed me a few coins. "Bring back as many as you can for that, and get one for yourself."

"Thanks, mate," I called and took his money. I was so tempted to run for it there and then—I didn't have much in my hand, but it was a start. But as I considered my next action, a black figure caught the corner of my eye. It was Marcus. So this was where he was. I entered the inn and headed towards the bar. I was a little smaller than the rest of the guests in there, so I could weave in and out of them without being too visible. Marcus had sat himself in a corner seat, as he had always done at The Four Keys. As I continued to head for the ale, I also saw the man that we had met on the dock earlier go and sit with him. Unfortunately I could not hear anything that was being said, so I got the ale, four tankards in total, and went back outside and gave it to the men there.

"Thanks, lad, you're a treasure," they all agreed. I declined to have one myself, but still stood there continuing to listen to the music.

"So have you been in port long?" I asked the man in the red coat.

"Just came in yesterday, and will be leaving again in two day's time," he replied.

"Regular haunt of your then this…the Weathered Man?" I nodded my head at the inn as I spoke.

"Aye, come here every time we land we do. Best ale in the town. We all have our favorite places to come to and this one is ours." He drank the full tankard of ale in one go, and snatched another off one of the other men who was too drunk to fight back for it so let it go easily.

"So you will know some of the people in there then…that is you being a regular…and me not being here before and wanting to know my way around." I waited for a reply as he downed the second tankard in one as well.

"Aye, I probably do so. So this is your first time here then? I thought so. You are too young to have spent long at sea. So just ask old Bill here and I'll tell you who is who and the like. And if I don't know I'll make something up that fits." He laughed as he spoke. It wasn't funny to anyone but to himself what he had said, but he was so full of ale that everything seemed to be.

"Say for example then, I wanted to know the names of all the captains of the ships around here then, who might they be?" I looked at him quizzingly.

"Well, starting from the top," he pointed them out as he spoke, "there is Captain Moore on the Moonshiner, a fast ship, but not as good as that of Captain John Blade on the Black Venture. This one here and the next one I am not too sure of, some sort of merchant ships, going to New England I think. But that next one is the Rescuer owned by Captain Sammy Barrett, or Sammy Bull's Eye, as he is know, cos he never misses. The next one is one of his as well the Mermaids Purse. And the one next to the end well, the Captain of that isn't here at the moment, so its being watched by Willy, don't know his full name, everyone just calls him Willy Short on account of him not being too tall. Don't cross him though, he's a fearful fighter and looks like he's been raised from the dead. The ships named the Fearless and all the crew are certainly that—everyone keeps well away from them. And I'm with the one on the end the Gunnershot. You probably passed my captain when you went for the ale, Captain Pellant. There's a right mixture of pirates and normal sea folk here, but as long as we don't create any trouble, no one can get arrested, so we all mind our P's and Q's when in port. All got a job to do at the end of the day, and can do without any unnecessary complications such as a hanging." He laughed again to himself and carried on with the singing.

"Just one more question, Bill?" I asked, tugging at his sleeve to get him to acknowledge me.

"What's that?" he asked and leant over to me, the strength of his breath nearly knocking me out.

"Who is that in there? Is he a captain as well? He's dressed all fancy and carries two pistols and other weapons." From where I was standing outside, I could see Marcus's back through an open window, and pointed him out to Bill.

"Aye, everyone knows who that is. Its Marcus Fleet, he's the captain of the Fearless I mentioned earlier. Didn't think he was here, must have crept in when I wasn't looking, he seems to do that a lot for some reason, here one minute and gone the next. You don't want to be messing with him either though. We all stay well clear. Rumor has it he has never shed a single drop of his own blood in fight. Shots just pass straight through him, and knives don't cut his skin." He acted out the actions as he spoke. "I ain't ever seen him in action, cos no one does ever cross him, so I can't tell you if that is really true. But don't let you be the first to find out."

I thanked him kindly for his information and let him resume his singing.

I stood there a while longer watching Marcus through the window. Twice he looked around and straight at the spot where I was standing, but I managed to duck out of the way just in time to avoid his gaze. Had he sensed me? The other man who was with him I now knew to be Captain Pellant. He was laughing and joking, but Marcus resumed always a stern expression. Pellant's joviality must a got a little too much for Marcus at one stage, and he smashed his hand down hard on the table in obvious annoyance and anger. Pellant immediately stopped and seemed to grovel a little, looking now no longer friendly but extremely fearful. Marcus rose from his chair, and headed towards the back of the inn. I legged it as fast as I could back to the yard, and started to climb on the barrels. I saw him through the open back door head towards the stairs; he was obviously going back to our room. As fast as I could, with my heart pounding, I pulled myself back in through the open window and tried to untie the sheets. My hands were shaking, but I finally managed it. I heard the key in the lock. The door opened, and Marcus entered to find me lying in exactly the same position as I had been in when I had first fallen to sleep.

Chapter 17
Gambling

For the next few hours until dawn had fully awaken, Marcus took his seat by the window and again watched the alley. It was the other window he could do with watching, I thought to myself, as that is the one that someone could easy climb in and out of. I drifted back in and out of sleep, but never fell fully fast, and Marcus was always awake every time I looked at him. Did he ever sleep?

With the break of the day, it had brought fresh activity to the street. The drunks were thrown out of the inns and the doors locked. Those that had not made it ashore laughed at them as they all staggered down the street, trying to remember which ship they were from. The hustle and bustle of the day's trading started again, and barrels and crates where carried on and off ships. Marcus finally moved from his seat. He straightened his coat and hat and unlocked the door.

"Come, Sam, we are going out. You can leave your stuff here, we will be back later," he said.

"Are we stopping here then?" I asked.

"Maybe for just one more night. It's not to my liking to get familiar, but it depends if Pellant has got my money." He walked out of the door, and waited in the corridor for me to follow so that he could lock the room behind us. He gave me the key, and I placed it in my pocket. I followed him down the dark corridor and out through the back door. We walked down the side alley, that he had sat watching all the time, and rounded the corner onto the street. It was going to be a nice day today, a good one for sailing. The sun was rising well and warming the air pleasantly and there was a southwesterly breeze building up which would help the ships leave port. I looked at all the vessels as we strolled down by the harbor wall. A couple flew English flags, a red cross on a white background. These were the ones that had been pointed out to me as the merchant ships, but the rest declined to display any colors. Most of the sails were gathered up and tied with ropes, just like the ones that Old Tom used to have in his cottage, and the rest just flapped around loosely in the wind.

Part way down the street Marcus stopped and handed me some coins. "Go and get yourself something to eat, if you get in any trouble say that you are with me, and I can be found on the Gunnershot. But otherwise I don't want to see you until noon." And he quickly strode off. I was just about to shout, "Where?"—but he had gone, vanished into the crowd.

Surveying my surroundings, I saw that there were several places where I could buy food. I walked over to their windows and peered inside. Each establishment was cooking its own specialties. Instead of the large open hearth that we had had at The Four Keys, they cooked over large oblong grates from which spits hung, roasting large joints of meat. They had supports, which swung out over the fire from which to hang several large pots. I could see their lids lifting and rattling with the boiling steam from their contents as small puffs of it would pop out erratically. At the side, on a table, lay fancy-shaped plates and cups, and knives and forks to eat with. I could hear people inside asking for brawn, chicken, savory black and white puddings and other such things. In another shop there were fancy-shaped loaves, gingerbread, and biscuits and spice cakes. Another served green pea soup, potted venison, and fish in pastry and potato pudding. I remembered my meager diet of eggs, vegetables and stew and my mouth watered at the thought of tasting something different. I felt like I had found my profession in life—to try out everything.

Entering the first place, I ordered some pancakes and marmalade. They were severed to me at a table of my own, with a chair of my own, and several utensils to use. I paid and sat looking at it for several minutes. The truth was I didn't really know which knife or fork to use first and how to use it. Luckily no one was watching so I just rolled it all up with my fingers and stuffed it into my mouth, until I could hardly shut my lips together. It tasted like pure heaven. That was it; I had to get more. I quickly rushed into the next shop, not having fully chewed and swallowed the food from the first place, and made my selection. Again I was directed to a table of my own. This time I had ordered some of the meat and vegetables. I didn't know what the recipes were called so had just sort of pointed at a few things that looked good. At least this time I was given a spoon as well when I got served, so it was a little easier for me to eat. My table was by the window, and as I ate I watched the ships getting ready to sail. I think I could be a sailor. I could get used to this life. It all seemed so perfect loading and unloading the ship, singing and eating.

However, my illusion was soon shattered when I saw through the shop window an argument taking place. One man pulled a pistol out and without hesitation shot the other. To my surprise no one took any notice of it, and the body was just pushed over the side of the harbor wall and let to drop into the sea. Maybe I wouldn't bother going to sea after all, and would become a cook or something else instead.

Fully stuffed with fine food, I left the shop and now sat on a make shift bench near the harbor wall and watched the waves. They gently swayed the boats back and forth, again and again, almost hypnotic. The warm sun beat down upon me and I started to daydream. Who was Marcus Fleet? He had marched into my life and smashed it apart, and now I was possibly on the run. Alright, I had intended on leaving The Four Keys but not quite in this fashion. He was obviously well known around here, and had been at sea a long time. But apart from an odd snip-it here and there, like about his cousin Isaac, I didn't know that much about him. The other sailors, or should I say, pirates, because that is what they really all are around here, seemed to stay well clear of him because of some tale which none of them had the guts to prove true. He dressed in the best clothes, carried himself well and was obviously well educated which I could tell from the way that he spoke. But despite his coolness, he also had a fiery side, and was used to getting what he wanted, and most of all, I still didn't fully understand how I fitted in to all this. I was the daughter of a cousin that he clearly didn't like, so why was he taking care of me. Was it because I had delivered his precious ring to him? Surely not. That had not been an intended action, I had just happened to have it at the time he was looking for it. What ever his reasons where, I finally decided not to let it bother me anymore and just tag along for the ride. It would all come out in the end, be it for better or for worse. This was the last time I was going to let myself be worked up by the situation; it was what it was.

"Sam, Sam," I heard a voice bellowing across to me. It was Marcus. He was swiftly striding off the Gunnershot. "Get off you backside and come over here." I did as I was told. "I want to you look at this man, Sam," he said and pointed back on ship to Captain Pellant. "This is the face of a robber and a swindler, don't you ever do any dealings with him. He'll rob the pennies of your dead grandmother's eyes given half the chance." I didn't know at first whether to take this seriously or not, only the other day he had been his best friend joking and laughing, but now Marcus seemed to be very angry.

"Be gone yourself, it's the other way round," Pellant called back, and threw him a small black leather bag filled with coins, which Marcus caught with ease. A big grin grew across his face again, and his blue eyes twinkled. Thank goodness for that, I didn't want to see another man being shot.

"I thank you most kindly," he called back and headed back up the street towards the Weathered Man. I ran after him, but he took some catching up as he walked so fast.

At the inn, he headed straight for the bar, ordered a full bottle of rum and took himself off into one of the dark corner's spots, and started to down it like it was water. As soon as it was empty, he ordered another, and drank that all down too. For the first time I actually saw him relax a little.

"Sam, don't you ever get to start drinking this stuff," he said and he waved the bottle in front of my nose. "It lives in your blood and you can't get rid of it. One sip and you are under its spell again. It's the devils drink, and I know it well. Be gone back outside with yourself and have another good look around, this might be the last that you see of the likes of this."

I didn't fully know what he meant by the last bit of his speech, but I nonetheless left the inn and went back outside into the sun. I could see from the corner of my eye, that he had slouched his position and was lying over the table looking either extremely drunk or was fast asleep. I hoped it was the latter.

For the rest of the day I walked up and down the street. I called in the baker's and spent the last of my money on some cakes and biscuits and found a fresh water well to gain a drink from. When the sun started to set, the work on the ships slowed down and I could see the captain's hands picking from the crew who was to be allowed on shore for the evening. The two merchant ships had left, and another was anchored out at sea. The wind from the morning had completely dried out, and the sea was as still as pond. Only a small splash could be heard now and then as it kissed the harbor wall. Time to head back to the inn, I was getting a little tired.

The inn was generating a lot of noise. I could hear men cheering and calling. There was what appeared to be a large gambling match going on, and Marcus was in the thick of it. The tables in the room had all been pushed to the side and a few of the pirates, Captain Pellant and Marcus, were busy taking turns at throwing a dice. I pushed my way through the crowd until I got onto the front line of spectators. It didn't take long before the crewmen who had been gambling lost their money and dropped out. That just left Captain Pellant and Marcus. They continued rolling for a few coins at a time, first one winning and then the other, they seemed equally matched in their luck. But I wished he would stop it; that was our money that he was gambling, the money from the sale of the cart and its goods. I could see him taking the coins from the same bag that had been thrown to him that morning. More and more ale got drunk by the surrounding gang, and the more they drank the more they spurred Marcus and Pellant on. Pellant now seemed to have the winning streak, and Marcus's moneybag was going down.

"I bet you all this, for all that's left in your bag," Pellant said.

"You're on," said Marcus confidently. I had seen this scenario before at my old home, and confidence never won. I crossed my fingers and held my breath. Pellant rolled first a four. It was a middle of the road score. Marcus took the dice and rolled. In the room that was once filled with cheering, not a noise was heard, except that of the dice rolling along the floor. It hit the wall at the other end and bounced back. It landed—a three. Oh no, disaster. Pellant swanked over to Marcus and removed the black bag from him. Marcus did not flinch. His expression did not change.

"And now for the big one," said Pellant smoothing his beard as he spoke. "I'll bet you double all these winnings for that silver ring that you have." He slapped down all the coin bags that he had won on the nearest table. How did he know about the ring? Marcus always kept it under his glove. "I've won it before and I want it again," he growled. So that was it. Marcus must have lost it gambling before. That's why it had got parted from him. No doubt initiated by a few bottles of rum first. I just couldn't work these two out, they seemed to play each other off, pretending to be best mates, but all the time weeding each other's money from them.

"No," Marcus firmly replied. "This time the ring is not for playing with." He straightened his coat and turned to walk away.

"Is that so," said Pellant, and he drew his pistol and pointed it at Marcus's back.

"Shoot a man in the back, will you?" said Marcus.

"I'll shoot a man anyway up that pleases me to get that ring. Now hand it over. We've been mates for too long to let a tiny piece of silver get in our way. Just pass it to me and you can go on your way again just like last time." He slowly started to cock the pistol. Marcus turned around slowly.

"You know that while I wear the ring, you can't kill me," he said, and he pulled off his glove to prove it was there. The rest of the room was starting to empty.

"Aye, that may be so, not straight away." Pellant spoke slowly and continued to stoke the situation. "But you know how the ring works as well as I. As long as the stone is missing you won't die quickly, but you will die. And every drop of your blood that falls will hit the ground like a nail in your coffin. So be a good mate, and pass it to me then." Pellant held his hand out.

"I said no," Marcus repeated.

"Then this is the first of many nails to come."

Pellant fired his gun, but Marcus dived away quickly and rolled to the other side of the room. The shot still hit him, but instead of it being straight through the heart as Pellant had directed towards, it pierced his left shoulder.

"One shot gone, Pellant, is that the best that you can do?" Marcus teased him. Pellant drew his other pistol and fired it at him. This time Marcus had grabbed one of the inn's stools and managed to deflect the shot into the seat. "Two shots gone, Pellant, you don't get to three." And he drew his sword. Pellant was just as quick and drew his as well. The room had well cleared of the guests now except for a few foolhardy ones, and me. They fought each other with the blades, matching swing for swing.

"So then what happened to the stone, Marcus?" called Pellant. "Did you gamble that away as well? You could never hold your rum, or your pride."

"You know what happened to the stone, you stole it as well," replied Marcus, still circling the room.

"Aye, you are right, I did have it, prized it out of its holder with my own teeth. It was worth far more than the ring, and I was short of a penny or two at the time. There were many that wanted it, but none could hold it. It burnt the damn skin from my fingers. Look," and Captain Pellant held up his hand. It looked like he had put it in the fire. The skin from his fingers was clean burned away, and scarred back, you could nearly see his bones.

"That'll teach you to take things you're not supposed to have," said Marcus and he lunged at Pellant cutting a large slash through his upper arm. "And now you can have some nails as well," he said..

Chapter 18

The Blood Red Stone

The fight spilled out into the street. Both men lunged at each other, but both managed to avoid and reflect the advances. The blades of their swords glistened in the moonlight as they danced around. A few of the onlookers started to argue as to whom was going to win the fight and several other punch-ups ensued. I had followed them out into the street and watched with frightened anticipation. Both were now bleeding badly but it didn't slow them down. On the other side of the street I saw Bill, still in his dirty red coat, watching as well, and I made my way over to him.

"Why doesn't someone stop it?" I asked.

"It's not the pirate's way to get in the middle of two crossed blades," he replied.

"But they are going to kill each other." I tugged at his coat to make him take me on. But his eyes were permanently fixed on the two dueling men.

"No, lad," he finally said, "only one will die tonight, the other will last out for many days yet before the blood finally drains from his veins. You see, Marcus has the silver ring, it won't let him die from the blade. Not even a blow through the heart will make him fall. His blood will just drip away. Now if he had the stone as well then that would be a different story. I have heard tales of this ring before, but now I am seeing it with my own eyes, I know they are true." He continued to watch and moved down the street a little so that he could get a better view.

"But Pellant had the ring before, didn't he?" I said.

"Yes he did, but the powers of it didn't work for him, even when he had the stone as well. But he won't let it lie, he still thinks that it might work if he tries again. All that he got was burned hands from the blood red ruby. It's said that no mortal man can touch it except those of the family from were it came from." Bill told me this with seriousness in his voice.

"What happened to it then?" I asked.

"Pellant got the ring from Marcus in a drunken bet, won it fair and square, and then set to sea. But the ring didn't work for him, so he ripped the stone out with his teeth, on account that you can't touch it with your flesh as it will burn your skin away. He meant to sell it, but one of his crew stole it, a old fellow by the name of Tom or John, I think, any ways he skipped ship at the next port and no one saw him after that." Bill pushed several of the onlookers out the way so that he could get a bit closer.

"What does the ruby look like?" I asked, wondering if this Tom he referred to was the same one I had known.

"Its about the size of a large raindrop, and is of the deepest red. It don't look like a true ruby though, it's sort of cloudy in color."

Oh, it couldn't be, could it? It sounded just like the stone that I had found at the inn. I quickly put my hand into my pocket so see if it was still there. I had forgotten all about it. I felt the key from bedroom door, and then there at the very bottom I felt it, a small round stone. I pulled it slowly from my pocket and looked at it in my hand.

"Here," someone called out. "The lads got it. He's got the blood red ruby. Give it to me."

He tried to grab it, but only succeeded in knocking it from my grasp. It rolled on the floor into the crowd. Uproar out broke, and they all went wild all trying to grab it and keep it. But every time they touched it, it burned their skin and they instantly dropped it again. I fell to the floor and scurried around on my hands and knees trying to retake it every time it fell. Finally I managed to grab it—but found myself at the feet of Pellant.

"Well, well, well," he said and he lifted me up with my collar. "Seems like the lads cursed as well as you, Marcus." He glared at my face. "Don't I know you?" he said and ripped the scarf from my head. My hair fell over my face and gave me away. "I'll be blowed, it's the same little miss that you brought into town yesterday. So you was telling the truth when you said that you were related. Now then, this makes it a bit fairer fight in my direction I believe, Marcus. I got the girl and the stone; you only got the ring. You know the stone don't work without the ring, so I'll do you a deal. Give me the ring and I gets to keep the stone as well, and your little cross-dressing darling will go free."

Marcus stood there still with sword in defensive position. "Let the girl go free first and then I'll give you the ring."

"I will tell you what we will do. I takes the stone," and he rolled down his sleeve and beckoned for me to place it in his covered hand—which I did. "Now she can come and take the ring, but one false move and she gets it in the back." He placed his sword at the base of my spine and gently pushed me in Marcus's direction, but not losing contact with me at any time. Marcus started to loosen the ring.

"Don't you dare hurt her," he called, "she's got nothing to do with this." He passed the ring to me. But before I could turn and pass it to Pellant there was a loud smash, and a full bottle of rum had been smacked squarely over his head. Pellant fell forwards flat to the ground, completely knocked out. The stone rolled from his covered hand and stopped at Marcus's feet. Marcus swiftly picked it up. As we turned to where Pellant had once stood, there was Willy Short with a broken bottle in his hand and a big grin on his face.

"Couldn't stand the man," said Willy ever so matter of fact, and he then turned and ran, closely followed by a shouting bunch of men waving their swords at him, presumably Pellant's crew as Bill was amongst them.

"Quick," said Marcus and he grabbed my arm. "We've got to go, too many people know about the ring now."

We ran for our lives down the street to the end of the harbor and then weaved through a few of the back alleys. Marcus pulled me into a dark doorway and we stood there for a few moments to gain our breath. I could see an angry mob running up and down, cursing and swearing our names.

"What are we going to do?" I asked between pants.

"Can you ride a horse?" Marcus replied.

"No," I replied.

"Well, that makes two of us then." He pointed over to a few horses at the back of one of the establishments that were tethered with rope to a gate.

"No way," I said. But he took no notice and dragged me across. I could see that a couple of them were still saddled and reined and these were the ones he untied. He pushed me up onto one and leapt on the other himself.

"It can't be that hard—can it?" he cried, and slapped the horse firmly on the buttocks with the excess rein. It whinnied loudly, rose up onto its back legs and then started to gallop as fast as it could up the alley with Marcus clinging on for dear life. The crowd had heard the commotion of the horses and they started to flood down the alley towards me. There was no way that I was staying to face that mob on my own, so I did the same, found myself gripping the reins so hard that my knuckles turned white, and bounced up the alley after him.

Pirates were supposed to ride in ships, not on horses.

Chapter 19
Daniel

We galloped in to the night like a pair of rag dolls clinging onto the horses. They eventually slowed and we started to get the idea of how to steer and control them. Following the coastline we traveled north, but never lost sight of the sea.

Eventually Marcus brought the horses to a stop. They were sweating and panting, not unlike myself. I slid myself off the saddle and collapsed onto the long grass. Every part of my body ached. My bones had been shaken so much by the riding; they felt like they were no longer joined together. Marcus gently got himself down as well, and sat beside me.

"Do you believe in the power of the ring?" I asked him.

"Well, it didn't do me much good last night, did it?" he replied, laughing and started to remove his clothing. "Still managed to get shot." He peeled his jacket and shirt away at the shoulder to reveal his wound. The shot had hit in the left upper arm, but had passed straight through. It was a clean wound, but it still bled, slowly. His other cuts had only been minor flesh wounds and not as bad as first looked. He removed one of the ribbons that was slung around him holding his pistol and started to wrap it around the wound. But he was having difficulty in tying a knot.

"Here, let me help," I said and went to his assistance. As I wound the ribbon further around his arm, I could see on part of his shoulder blade that there were tattoos of several ships and the names of each neatly scribed underneath. All the markings were in black ink, only a single red flag, which was flying on each, broke the color. I finished tying the make shift bandage and it seemed to hold the blood flow.

"Thanks," he said softly, "can't feel a thing now, it's as good as new." He smiled at me gently.

We both lay and slept on the grass until the sun had broken fully. We were too worn out to have done anything else, and had any of the other pirates managed to follow us, we would have been right easy pickings for them.

"Marcus," I said, "why are you doing all this? All this running and plotting for the sake of a silver ring which everyone thinks is cursed or has some sort of special powers." I put my hand into my pocket and removed the ring. It was a very simple piece, heavy in weight, that had not a cut or scratch mark upon it. I studied it for a few moments and then passed it to Marcus. He placed it upon his finger and looked at me.

"The tale I told you about your parents…there is a little more to it than that. The ring and you are just part of it." He continued, "My father William argued dreadfully with Isaac, you remember my cousin, all the time about his womanizing. Isaac is a few years older than me, and was annoyed that the family estate would not become his one day. But that's the way that lifelines and hereditary estates work. He had lived with us from being small after his own father, my uncle, my father's younger brother, had died, and granted he had worked hard on the land to make it profitable. When your birth had came to light, that was the final straw for my father, they paid for Jacob to leave with you, Maggie and Daniel and therefore get rid of any blemishes on the family name all in one go. But they argued terribly one night, and Isaac hit him. I was in the room, but being only 15 could not over power him. My father fell and hit his head as he landed. I rushed to his aid but blood was pouring out from his wound. I tried to stop it, but it was useless and I just became covered in it. Isaac saw what had happened and locked me into the room with my father, shouting that he was going for the authorities to arrest me for my father's murder. It would have been a perfect way for him to inherit the family's estate. I panicked, stole the ring from my father's writing desk, and climbed out the window and down the balcony. I thought that I would be able to sell it for a few shillings and have some money to live on. But instead of being met by the authorities, I was met by two rough-looking sailors, was gagged and carried away to work on a pirate's ship as a lower deck hand. I later found out that Isaac had had this planned all along, and knowing that I could not return back as a pirate or I would have been hanged, declared me dead at sea, lost on a misadventure. He inherited my estate and this is where we are." He was very solemn when he spoke about his father, and angry when he mentioned Isaac.

"So, you can't claim back your estate, because people think you are dead. And if you do turn up, they will see that you are a pirate and have you hanged. So what about me?" I asked.

"Well, you, my dear, are going to get the estate back for me. When I get Isaac declared the murderer of my father, then you are the only living blood relative. I will have him write a will declaring you the beneficiary, and the courts will turn the land over to you."

"But why? Why bother after all this time, and why involve me?" I questioned.

"I had to wait until you was of a legal age or else I would have done this years ago. How do you think all this has been for me?" He snapped at me. "Living at sea for all these years, originally a gentleman and now a pirate. My life has not exactly been a bed of roses. But I swore that I would revenge my father's death and bring out the true murderer."

"And why didn't you get rid of the ring, sell it or something?"

"Because I remembered that it was a family heirloom, and I remembered all that my father had told me about it, and I would need to keep hold of it if my plan was to work." He turned his back to me and stood up. "Time we were going. The horses are knackered, they'll be no use to us now." He drew his pistols and shot them both. After all those tender words he had quoted me about his father, how could this man be such a hardened killer. He didn't seem to care if anything got in his way, he just shot it, had his compassion been lost over the years or he had always been like this?

After several hours of trudging through the open country, we came across farmland. Several herds of cows and sheep mixed freely in fields and chewed the grass. There was a large hay barn, and a large farmhouse, which had several smaller out buildings attached for keeping pigs and the like.

"Can you ride a cow? Because I have another plan," Marcus asked.

"You have got to be joking," I replied. But this time he was, and he laughed out loud.

"I had you there, didn't I?" he continued to laugh. He certainly had, but I wouldn't have put it past him. "Here, go and see if you can buy some bread and milk from them, I'll wait here." He passed me a few coins and then crouched down behind the surrounding wall. I jumped over and ran down to the front door. I knocked and a kind-looking lady came and indicated for me to go around the back. After a couple of minutes she came with a small bundle, a small churn and took my money. I headed back to the wall were Marcus was hiding. She had given me a small amount of cheese, a couple of apples, some freshly baked bread, as it was still warm and some fresh milk. Marcus took a small portion, muttered that he would rather have had some rum, and gave the rest to me. I didn't eat it all, but saved a little for later. Since he had put the ring back on, his arm seemed strangely to have made a rapid recovery, and we were soon on our way again.

Five miles down the road was a solitary inn. It reminded me of The Four Keys. It fronted the coast and several small boats were moored. I presumed them to be fishing boats as most contained nets and crab baskets. We went in, and Marcus headed predictably straight for a corner. There were several men already sat there, but when they saw him coming, they picked up their ale, moved rapidly and huddled together.

"I don't want no trouble in here," the lady keeper said, removing the empty dishes that had been left. "My name is Madge and if you want anything, just call or send the lad." She pointed at me. "I would be pleased if you would keep your troubles to yourself, we are a quiet inn, and your sort is not welcome, but I won't refuse your money if it is as good as everyone else's". Marcus nodded and she left us. She reminded me of my old Ma, round and plump, must be a characteristic of the position, as all the ladies I had seen serving had been of that same body shape.

Marcus sat in silence, not saying a word, but just kept drumming his fingers on the tabletop and kept looking at the door. He would stop when someone came in, but start again after he had seen who they were. I sat there in silence too. Looking around the room, I could see that the other guests were fishermen. They carried no weapons, well at least not like the sort that Marcus carried, and smelt of fish. They kept looking in our direction and it made me feel uneasy. But other than that they seemed to carry on with their own business. They drank, ate and chatted quietly, as there was no music or gambling like what the pirates did. Marcus finally stopped his drumming and called Madge over.

"A pint of ale for me please, and a glass of milk for the lad," he said. Madge went and brought the goods back. At least he hadn't ordered rum; I didn't want a repeat performance of the other night.

"You both from round here?" she asked. "You look sort of familiar."

"I was once here a long time ago," replied Marcus, "but Sam has never been here before." And with that answer she left us alone. Marcus continued to sit in silence and drum his fingers.

"Will you stop it," I said, "it's getting on my nerves. It's like you're drumming up a firing squad." His fingers had constantly rapped the same tune, 1-2-3, 1-2-3, 1-2-3, gap, 1-2-3, 1-2-3, 1-2-3, gap, over and over again. He looked at me, his eyes didn't seem to be as blue, and looked a little dark, perhaps he was tired. I also noticed that he had put the ruby stone back into the ring.

"Did the stone fit in alright then?" I asked. "It must have been the right one I found. What's the chances of that then, must be a thousand thousands to one, or more maybe, funny that…"

"Yes, thank you," he interrupted me. "They are drawn together eventually," he said, and finished his ale.

With the talk of the ring, a few of the fishermen pointed towards us again, and then turned and whispered to each other. Finally one of them got up and came to our table.

"Excuse me, squire," he said "but if you don't mind, we would like you to leave now. A few of us is not too happy about you being here. We knows that all pirates are not the same, and some are good, and we are hoping that you are one of them, and will kindly go. 'Tis just that you do seem familiar to us, and that ring you wear, well a similar one has been talked about a long time ago. We feel like we don't want you here now, so if you don't mind…" but he didn't finish his speech. Marcus slung his tankard down hard upon the poor man's hand crushing his bones, and then pressed it in further. The man fell to the floor, rolling around in agony.

Marcus hissed at them. "Fisherman's tales will be the death of you all. Don't cast your net without knowing the truth first, or you might catch something evil from the deep."

"Leave Charlie alone," called another, "or else…or else…" and he grabbed a chair and raised it above his head, "you will be beaten out of here."

"Aye," jeered the rest of the fisherman and they stood up, picking up various implements, and headed towards our table.

"Quick, Marcus, let's go," I said, jumping up ready to leave.

"I will go when I am ready," he slowly replied, and let them come a few paces closer.

As they all stood there staring at Marcus, the door of the inn suddenly opened and another man entered. He was about 20 years old and wore a hooded-riding cape, which he removed when entering. Seeing what was happening, he headed between the advancing crowd and Marcus.

"Stop it, gentleman," he called, "this is a friend of mine."

"Don't look like the type of friend you should have, Dan."

"I'd lose him if I was you," said another fisherman, and they backed off.

"I think we had better go, Marcus," said Dan.

We rose and started to leave. Dan? Had I heard right? Could this be Daniel, my brother? After all Marcus did know him. I bit my lip to stop me saying anything until I was totally sure, I had had so many of my memories smashed already, I didn't want to have any more false hopes.

The fishermen stood around the door as we exited, Dan first, then me, then Marcus. Charlie, the man whose hand was smashed, was cursing and few of the others had to hold him back. But he broke free and lunged at Marcus with a small fishing knife. He plunged it into Marcus's back, which made him stop and stand still for a moment. But as Charlie pulled it back out, his hand began to shake as he looked at the blade, and he dropped it on the floor. Not a speck of blood was to be seen.

Chapter 20

New Home

Dan had traveled to the fishermen's inn by way of horse and cart. Thank goodness, I couldn't have walked much further as my legs were tired, and I certainly couldn't have ridden anywhere on a horse as my backside was burning, and starting to blister from my earlier attempt. Marcus jumped up front of the cart with Dan and I climbed onto the back.

"Have a sleep," Marcus said to me, "it's going to be a while before we get home." I curled up under some sacks and old covers in the back of the cart, making myself as comfortable as I could. Marcus and Dan chatted quietly to each other, their voices low so that I could not hear what was being said. The rocking of the cart on the road soon had hypnotized me to sleep.

The next thing I knew, Marcus was shaking me to wake me up. "Come on, sleepy, we are here," he muttered. The evening had well drawn in now and the horse and cart had been stopped outside a small stone cottage. Was this it? Was this Marcus's great estate, it wasn't worth arguing over if it was. I got down from the cart and entered the little cottage. There were the remains of a fire just about glowing in the hearth, but the room was not cold so it didn't need to be restarted straight away.

Dan showed me to a small room off the main living area. I was desperate to say something and see if he was my brother. But in over four years we had both no doubt greatly altered in appearance, and the light was dim now so we couldn't see each other's faces in too much detail. The room contained a small bed, complete with proper bed linen and a blanket. There was also a small chair and a dressing table with two large drawers. Dan had given me a lighted candle so I could see my way, which I placed upon the table. There were no pictures or ornaments except for a large china washing bowl and jug filled with very cold water. A small piece of soap and a towel lay beside it. It was almost as though he had been expecting a visitor. The window in the room was bolted, but was made from proper glass, not a wooden shutter as I had been used to. Apart from the brief stay at the Weathered Man, this was the only other time I had been given a proper bed to sleep in, and I also here had a room to myself. I could still hear Marcus and Dan discussing things outside the room, and felt it best if I left them alone. Although I had slept well on the way here, it wasn't long before I was undressed, curled up in the bed and fast asleep once more. Even though I was again in a strange place, I can truly say that this was the first night for a long time that I slept completely, solidly and well.

The morning broke and with it brought a fresh excitement for me. I felt quite safe here, so I leisurely washed myself and dressed slowly. When I left my room, the dawn rays of sun were shining in through all the windows of the cottage. It really was the prettiest place I had ever seen. Outside I could see rose vines entwined around bent fences. Wild flowers were growing and blooming all over the place. The main living area was simple but adequately dressed. It had a large table, which obviously doubled as a workbench as there were several carpentry tools placed at one end. There were four chairs placed around the table, a large sideboard and a rocking chair near the fire. A mirror hung on the wall, and also several small sketches of the coastline in home made frames.

"Sit down, Sam," said Marcus and he pulled a chair out for me. Rather gentleman like, I thought. "Dan's had to go out on some chores as he's the gardener here at the estate and doesn't want to be seen to be missing and therefore draw unwanted attention. Isaac is quite a time keeper and if his staff are late, he will call at their estate houses to find out where they are." So there was more to the estate then, and quite sizeable if all the staff had their own houses in the grounds. "He made this for you before he went," and Marcus placed before me a large bowl of hot porridge and a plate containing bacon, eggs and bread.

"Marcus," I tentatively started to say, "I've got to ask you, is Dan my brother Daniel? It seems too much of a coincidence that you know all about him and then at your estate a young man who fits his age and description appears."

"You are no fool, are you, Sam?" he laughed. "Yes, he is."

That was all I wanted to hear. I ate my breakfast with the largest smile possible on my face. It tasted wonderful and even more so knowing that he had made it. Alright, he was not my true blood brother, but he was most dear to me. I could not wait until he got back to tell him who I was. I was still dressed as a lad, and now wished that I had my stolen dress with me so that I could put it on for him. The last four years had seen great changes in my looks so it was forgivable that he had not spotted me straight away, I was only twelve the last time he had seen me. I finished my food in no time and jumped up from the table.

"Come on then, Marcus, let's go and find him," I beamed as I spoke.

"No, we can't, that will give us all away. He will be back soon enough, and in the meantime I will take you for a short walk through the grounds so you can see the house properly, but we must not be seen. It shouldn't be too bad this early in the morning most of the staff are busy in the house. But nevertheless they can not under any circumstances find out about me yet."

I nodded in acknowledgement and we both left the cottage.

Dan's cottage seemed to be standing on its own. The others seemed to be in groups of three or four, I could tell from the streams of smoke that were rising up from behind patches of trees. Marcus was extremely careful and told me not to say a single word while we were out. He constantly kept looking around and we took a most unusual route around trees and along the boundary wall. He always kept himself in a semi-bent position, so I did the same. After a short while I could see a clearing through the trees ahead and Marcus lead me in that direction. There was another gate and stone wall and a road that led through. We kept close to the wall and followed it for a small distance. Eventually we stopped and Marcus bobbed his head up over the wall. He beckoned for me to do the same. Once I was stood up I was overwhelmed with the vastness of the expanse of land that lay before me. Green field, followed on after green field. Some fenced with wooden posts and some not. Deer frolicked freely between the large oak trees and pheasants ran around without a care in the world. There were large perfectly shaped trees lining a road that ran as straight as a raindrop could fall. It ran from the gate we had passed up the hill and neatly into a large open courtyard, which lay before the largest house I had ever seen. Made from a light-colored stone, it had row upon row of windows, side by side, and above each other. It was a magnificent property, no wonder Marcus wanted to fight to have it back.

"Well, that is Flatt Manor," he said, "what do you think about it?"

I was still awestruck but managed to get out, "It's beautiful."

"Come on, we had best get back, before the grounds men start their rounds." And we turned and made our way back to Dan's cottage.

Chapter 21

Catching Up

Although we only waited a short time for Daniel to come back, it seemed like a whole day. I paced around the table and kept looking out of the cottage windows. The more I saw nothing, the more impatient I got. I just wanted to run out of the place and find him. Marcus's face was the picture of calmness. He sat in the rocking chair, but hardly moved it. His hands were placed upon his lap and his fingers were doing the same drumming motion that he had done in the last inn we went to. At least this time there was no noise as his fingertips rhythmically patted down up on his legs. So we both waited in complete silence.

Finally the deafening quietness was disturbed as Daniel flung open the cottage door, making me jump out of my skin.

"I've just called back to see if everything is alright, I've only got a few minutes, I am supposed to be trimming the main entrance hedges," he said as he entered.

I could hold myself back no longer. "Daniel," I yelled as I hurled myself at him and clung so tight around his neck that he could hardly speak. He tried to push me away a little in order that he could breath again, looking rather surprised at my sudden outburst.

Finally Marcus spoke, "Daniel, this is Samantha."

Daniel finally managed to break free from me. He glanced me up and down still looking rather puzzled. I pulled my headscarf off and my hair fell over my face and shoulders, making me look a little more like a lady and not a lad.

"Sammy, is that really you?" It felt so good to hear him call me that. No one else called me that except him. I nodded. My smile filled my face and my eyes sparkled with teardrops of happiness. "Sammy…I don't believe it…thank you, Marcus, thank you." This time he grabbed me and hugged me so tight I thought my back was going to break.

"I'll leave you two to catch up, I want to have another look around the old estate, it's been so long since I was last here." And Marcus left us.

Daniel brushed the hair from my face and stroked my cheek. His hands were a little rough, but I didn't care; they felt like velvet to me. He wiped my tears away so gently that I wanted to cry some more so he could do it again. Eventually we both let go of each other and sat at the table.

"Daniel, where have you been for the last four years? Why did you leave me alone with Ma and Pa at the inn? Why didn't you take me with you?" I had so many questions to ask.

Daniel pulled away from me a little and took a deep breath. "Has Marcus told you why you are here?"

"Yes, yes," I replied impatiently, I wanted to know about him not me.

"Then his plan has begun." Daniel rose from the table and started to pace around the room.

"I know that I am Isaac's illegitimate daughter. I know that Marcus wants his estate back because Isaac killed his father and had Marcus carted off to sea. But surely now he is here he can sort all that out, all I care about is that I have found you again—alive. I have been so worried." I started to cry again.

"Don't cry," said Daniel and he wiped my tears away again. His tone of voice soothed me and I stopped weeping.

"Tell me, Daniel, where have you been, why did you go?" I pleaded.

"Alright, but you might not be happy with what I have to say, especially about Pa who isn't as good as we thought." I knew that bit alright, but listened carefully as he continued.

"When we were very young, do you remember moving into the inn?"

I nodded.

"Do you remember seeing the broken boat at the bottom of the cliff?"

I nodded again.

"Well, that boat belonged to the owner of the inn. It was his house, only it was a fisherman's lodge then. Maggie took a liking to it and wanted it, so Pa..." he hesitated a moment, " fought the old fisherman and threw him off the cliff. To make it look like a fishing accident, he dragged the boat up the cliff and threw that off as well. I saw it all. I bit my lip and said nothing for many years, but finally one evening now that Pa had turned to drink, he used to be sober as a judge before that fateful night, he called me lazy and many other names I don't want to repeat and started to beat me, egged on by Maggie. He dragged me outside and part way up the cliff out of earshot of the inn. I feared for my life thinking that he might be throwing me off as well, and angrily said that I knew the truth about him and how he had killed the old man and if he didn't let me go I would report him. This just made him beat me all the more. But he was so drunk that he finally couldn't support his own weight and fell to the floor. Old Tom had followed us out that night and hid behind a rock. He came to my rescue and took me to his home in the wood. He cleaned me up and said that because of what I had said about Pa murdering the fisherman, if I didn't get out of here quick he would come back after me. He told me to wait at his cottage and he would sort something out. In the early hours of the morning, he brought Marcus back and he took me to work on one of his ships. Pa came looking for me the next morning, but I had gone. He knew Tom had done something but couldn't work out what. Marcus had been in the inn that night and knew Tom from old so he agreed to help, but Tom had to in turn help him and be his spy on land. Tom was in an ideal place to listen to the pirates' tales and pass the latest information back to Marcus." Daniel grabbed my hands and held on to them tight, "I am so sorry, that I left without saying good bye, but, you see, I just had to go straight away."

I looked down at the floor of his cottage, and squeezed his fingers in acknowledgment of his tale.

"There's a bit more to it now," I said. "I've settled into the idea that Ma and Pa are not my real parents, but Pa was your true father, and I am afraid to have to tell you that he's now dead himself."

Daniel looked at me shocked.

"He fought Old Tom over Marcus's ring, as he had found it, accused him of stealing and they both ended up on the cliff, and with the same fate as the fisherman. Ma accused me of their murders, but it was nothing to do with me honest, they both just fell, but luckily for me Marcus turned up good for me as he did for you."

I waited for a response off Daniel.

He turned his head away from me. "I'm so sorry, Sammy, it's all come to this. Don't worry about Pa and me. I always knew that Maggie wasn't my real mother, so I care not for her, and after the way Pa had treated me when I left, I care not for him either. Happen best that he has gone, as there is no telling what I might have done if I had seen him again." He produced a weary smile for me, but it made me feel a little better. "We can get on with our own lives now, Sammy. Did you say that Marcus had found the ring? I had heard that he had lost it again in a drunken bet."

"Yes, that's right. I found the stone a few weeks ago by sort of accident, and Old Tom found the silver ring. He's got it back now and wears it under his glove. I've heard a few strange tales about it, and met a few strange folk wanting to take it. Do you know anything about it? It seems to be very important to Marcus."

Dan replied, "When I first met Marcus, he had the ring, an old family heirloom he said. It's not decorated fancy and doesn't look worth much, if it had been he wouldn't have been allowed to keep it as you know what a reputation pirates have for gold and jewels. He told me how he had ended up at sea and worked his way up to captain of his own fleet, that's were he gets his name from, Flatt became Fleet. Got every ship he's commanded tattooed down his spine. But for a ring that's not worth a lot, he keeps it constantly hidden under a glove."

"Well, I heard that as long as he wears it, he can't be killed, and several other people I've met have agreed with this tale too," I said.

"I can't say if that is true or not," replied Dan. "I only actually spent two years at sea with him and spent most of that being sick, just never got my sea legs, so Marcus put me on shore and persuaded the old gardener who used to work here to give me a job. He remembered my Pa and kindly took me on. Passed away over a year ago and now I am head gardener in his place. I must say though that there was a few times in battle that I saw a shot or a blade pass in his direction and thought to myself that he must be a goner, only to see him pick himself up and carry on without a scratch. Must just be lucky I expect, he is very good fighter, never lost a fight yet."

"Maybe it's just in folks' minds that the ring is possessed. Imagination can be a powerful thing. I held the stone and it didn't do anything to me, but all the other pirates were convinced that it burnt them. Probably spent too long at sea and drunk too much rum to be able to separate the truth from fantasy anymore." I laughed as I spoke and Daniel chuckled too. "So did you see exotic islands and dolphins and whales and riches beyond belief, Daniel?"

"Aye, and much more than you could ever imagine. It was a hard life at sea, but a wonderfully exciting one."

I could see as he spoke that his mind was wandering back in time remembering all those fabulous things.

"Marcus has been a good friend to me, and I promised in turn to be the same to him." Daniel was suddenly flung back into present time as the clock he kept in his bedroom stuck the hour. "Is that the time? I've got to get back, I just hope I haven't been missed." He swirled around quickly. "I'll tell you all about it later, Sammy." And he grabbed the door handle and swung it wide open.

"No, Dan, tell the lady about it now," boomed a deep voice.

There in the doorway stood a rather portly looking man of around 45 years of age, I guess his figure doing justice to the fact that he obviously led a good rich life. "Tell the lady what a criminal you are, how you spent years at sea being a pirate, thieving, robbing, killing and raping no doubt. Tell her what an odious character you are. Tell her how lucky you are to have a friend like me who keeps you busy and on the good road away from trouble." He wafted into the house.

All the time he spoke, he flicked a small white handkerchief edged with delicate lace around in the air. He wore a long blue velvet coat, with a run of gold buttons all down the front, which were repeated on his matching satin waistcoat. They were close fitting, but the buttons peeped open where he had forced his large size inside. A gold embroidered cravat was loosely tied under his fat chin. Breeches gave way to stockings and his shoes were small and buckled neatly at the side, and on his head he wore the most dreadful white wig. It had obviously been over wheat powdered as whenever he moved, small specks fell off and left a light dusting where ever he went. His nose was large and bulbous and his eyes shifty and small.

"Well, Dan…cat got your tongue?" he asked in a most undermining tone.

"No, sir," replied back Dan, looking away from his face. "I am just back up to the top garden to finish the pruning now, sir."

"No, Dan, you must introduce me first to this scruffy little wench that dares to impose her presence in one of my cottages."

"This, sir, is Sammy, er…Samantha my sister. This, Samantha, is Lord Flatt, Lord Isaac Flatt."

Well, I would have rather bitten my tongue off there and then, than confess that this hideous man was my natural father.

Chapter 22

The Lord's Ghost

We both stood there staring at each other. Lord Flatt's tone of voice changed as he asked, "Tell me, young lady, what is your full name?"

"Samantha Alice Battle," I replied a little hesitantly.

"And what is your date of birth?"

"February the first 1700," I quietly whispered. I felt like I didn't really want to talk to him, and only answered to be polite.

"Are you quite sure?" he asked.

"Of course," I snapped back at him.

He stood there motionless, looking at me as though he had seen a ghost. Then he let out the most awful cry. His fingers began to twitch and move erratically, and started to tear at his tatty wig, his knuckles all white with tension. The color completely drained from him. "My past has come back to haunt me," he wailed. "Lord, save me, my past has come back." He scurried out of the house quickly still wailing.

I stood there not knowing what to do. What did this all mean?

"Quick," said Daniel. "You are in danger and must go quickly. Run through the trees and get onto the main road, I'll try and locate Marcus and get him to get you away from here. It was not a good idea of his to bring you back."

He pushed me towards the door, and despite my persistent attempt to stay, he managed to force me outside. But it was too late. Lord Flatt had not ventured down to the cottage on his own, and I was grabbed on each arm by two of his footmen. A third blocked the doorway so that Daniel could not get out, and I was dragged towards the main estate house kicking and screaming. Daniel could do nothing to help; he could only look on.

Partway up the long driveway to the house, I decided that I wasn't going to get away by protesting and it was only tiring me out. So I started to walk properly the remainder of the journey, but the two men still did not let me go. Neither of them spoke except to say, "That's better, Miss," when I had decided to behave myself, and neither of them looked at me, they just kept staring ahead at the house and Lord Flatt. He had also calmed down now and was striding the rest of the way like a proper gentleman. I had took an instant dislike to him, father or not, and wanted to spit at him.

At the entrance to the house, my guards released me. My arms were sore where they had held on tightly and I rubbed them to ease the pain. They still accompanied me inside and firmly closed the door behind us all. Only now did they give me a little room to move.

Lord Flatt had regained his pompous attitude, and waved his handkerchief at a couple of serving maids. They instantly came to his aid and helped him remove his coat. His wig still sat crooked upon his head from when he had been clutching it at Daniel's cottage, but no one mentioned it to him. They were either all too afraid, or were leaving it like that to make him look foolish, and I wasn't going to say anything too. I looked around the room that I was in. It was only an entrance hall, but it was bigger than the ground floor of any of the other buildings I had ever been in. The floor was tiled with marvelous colored squares in a most uniform pattern. A large staircase lay straight ahead of me, made of marble and highly polished dark wood. Life size portraits hung on every wall in gilt frames, with hardly a gap between them. Some of them looked really old and the clothes were most unusual. I turned around to see them all, and my eye was cast upon Lord Flatt's ghost.

There hanging above a doorway was a picture of a young girl of around 20 years old. Wearing a white dress of the most delicate fabrics, she was sat at a table reading a book. She was an exact double of me. Her name was written underneath and there were some numbers also. I couldn't read them except for one word 'Alice'. I knew this from my own name. My own name was the only thing I could read. Daniel had taught me this. He had managed to go to school for a few years as it was thought proper that boys could read and write. It wasn't thought necessary for girls. At least this lady in the picture had managed to get an education, and was obviously from a very wealthy family. Only wealthy families could have portraits painted like these ones.

Lord Flatt came over to me and noticed that I was looking at this painting. "She's very pretty, isn't she?" he whispered down my ear.

I nodded.

"Do you see a resemblance to yourself…you should, she was my mother…your grandmother." So he did know who I was then. But why was he treating me so horribly? He waived his handkerchief again at some more servants, and two different girls, only young this time, came and stood by me. "Take her to the Seaview guest room and find her some more suitable clothes…and oh…get her washed first."

The two girls led me up the staircase and to the right. We went down a long corridor and stopped at the end room. There was a key in the door, which they used to open it, and we all went inside. I was beginning to think that none of the servants spoke around here, but as soon as we were inside the room and the door closed the two girls didn't shut up.

"Hello, Miss, my name is Sally and this Jayne." The other girl curtseyed to me to acknowledge her name. "This room ain't been used for a long time by the looks of things." Sally went to open the curtains and Jayne pulled back the covers on the bed. There was a light layer of dust over everything and it rose into the air as they busied around, floating in the sunbeams flowing in from the window. "We'll soon have this all clean for you," Sally continued, "and then you can have a nice bath and change those clothes."

I sat myself down in a seat near the window and looked out whilst the girls cleaned and dusted the room. Seaview was a good name for the room. I hadn't realized how high up on land we were on this estate. In the far distance was the thin silver twinkling line of the ocean. The girls chatted away to each other as they worked, no doubt talking about me as they kept glancing in my direction. I just sat there and stared out the window, scanning the grounds to see if I could see Daniel or Marcus, but there was no one I recognized.

"Miss, Miss," said Jayne.

I turned to her voice.

"We are just going to go and get you some water for a nice bath, won't be long, just you stop here please."

I nodded, and as they both left, and I heard the door being locked from the outside. Was he going to keep me a prisoner here? Not if I could help it. I stood and went to the window. The locks were stiff but I managed to open it. Sticking my head out I could see that I was directly over the front courtyard, and also that it was a sheer drop down to it. No way I could climb out of this window then! I pulled it shut and went and lay on the bed. The ceiling in the room was painted white and had a plaster design of leaves and swirls upon it. I was letting my eyes follow them around aimlessly when suddenly the door was unlocked and a whole procession of servants came in with pails of warm water and poured them into a bath that was placed behind a screen. Sally and Jayne remained in the room with me and the door was locked again, this time from the outside. Jayne was holding a pale blue dress in her hands, which she laid down on the bed.

"If you would, Miss, please have a bath and put this dress on after. We will wait here to give you any help that you need, master's orders." Sally and Jayne backed off a little and stood to one side, holding their hands together in front of them.

"Oh, sit yourselves down, you're making me nervous," I said.

They both smiled at me and ran for the same chair near the window. They pushed and shoved each other but finally Sally got into it first. Jayne pulled herself a stool up near it and they both looked out the window. It made me chuckle a little to see them tussling in their long dresses, it was something I used to do with Daniel at home before he left, but without the dresses of course. They both only looked a similar age to me, and here they were, signed to a life of serving, when they should have been out in the sun having fun. I know that I had been put to work at The Four Keys, but at least

I got to go out regular and wasn't shut in all day. Their skin was very pale, unlike mine, which had a deep golden tan. I rose from the bed and went behind the screen. The bath was a funny shape, but the water was warm and a good wash was something that I desperately needed.

The water was warm, and caressed my aching tired body. The girls continued to giggle and act like a couple of children, pushing and pinching each other.

"Have you both worked here long?" I asked.

"Yes, Miss," came back the surprising answer from Sally. "I've been here for about six years, first in the kitchen and now as one of the maids, and Jayne has been here for about four years; she started a little after me. We are sisters, but we don't look alike, Miss, good job too. The master doesn't like families working here, so we go by different surnames. Here, you won't tell, will you?" This last question was prompted by a sharp jab in the ribs by Jayne when she had mentioned that they were sisters.

"No," I replied. "It's no concern of mine. I just want to get out of here!"

"What the bath?" said Sally.

"No, this place, this house, this life." I got myself out of the water and took one of the large soft cloths that were now hanging over the screen to dry myself on.

"I don't know why, Miss," said Sally. "I'd give my left leg, and my right leg, if it came to it, to live in a house like this."

"It's not the house, the house is beautiful, it's Lord Flatt and this way of life, I'm just not used to it."

"Well, you had better get used to it, being his relative and the like. Here you are his long lost missing daughter, aren't you? Only you are the double of that portrait in the great hall, and I've heard all the rumors that are going around," asked Jayne.

"It would appear so. But he doesn't seem like the most approachable of men," I replied.

"That, I have heard is on account of his lost loves," said Sally. "His beloved uncle was killed many years ago by his own wicked son. It hurt the master so much that he swore that he won't rest until Mark Flatt has been found and hanged. But everyone knows that he was drowned at sea, but the master still has wanted posters out for his head."

So, that poster that Marcus had ripped down was really his, only now he was known as Marcus Fleet and not Mark Flatt. He had conveniently forgotten to tell me that, was there anything else that he had forgotten to tell me, or had twisted the truth about? I decided to quiz the girls more. They were only young and wouldn't know when they were speaking out of turn. All servants know all the gossip that goes around a house, perhaps they could tell me more.

"What did you hear about me?" I asked as I put on the blue dress. Sally came to help me fasten it up.

She replied, "The story is that you are the daughter of the master. He had an affair some 16 years ago with a maid from the house. The uncle wasn't too pleased, after all it's not right that the gentry mix with the servants, and he had you sent away. And just to annoy the master more, he sent you away with his one true love...Margaret I think her name was."

"Maggie," I butted in.

"That's right, Maggie she was known as to everyone. Master went mad, but calmed down quickly and forgave his uncle, but Mark was heard to think that it was all wrong and fought with his father, and killed him. Master has never been with another woman since that day." She pulled tight on the laces at the back of my dress and it momentarily took my breath away. This was like the tale that Marcus had told me, but not quite the same. I didn't know whom to believe anymore, if only Daniel was here, he was always full of common sense.

The clock on the dresser struck seven. The two girls finished what they were doing, and removed the wet cloths. They went to the door and knocked to be let out.

"Please don't tell on us, you seem like a nice person, and it's so good to have someone young in the house. Always full of fluffed up old women and dusty men," said Jayne.

“I won’t,” I said and gave them a big friendly smile.

“Good night, Miss,” they chorused together. The door opened and they both left.

Then I realized, that the door had not been locked again. That’s it. I could make a run for it. I put on my old jackboots, although Lord Flatt had given me a lovely dress to wear, and ribbons for my hair, he had not given me any foot attire. Must be a shoe thing with the Flatts! Not used to women’s feet. They looked funny at first, but when the skirt was pulled back down you couldn’t see them. I headed for the door, almost running. But to my dismay the same two gentleman that had kindly dragged me up here were waiting, and escorted me in silence down the stairs and into the dining room.

Chapter 23
Dinner

Parades of servants were scurrying up and down the hallway near the entrance hall. Some carried single plates and others carried large silver platters with large silver covers hiding their contents. I was pushed in the direction of one of the rooms which I found out when I had entered was a dining room. Lord Flatt was standing at one end of a very long, highly polished table that was surrounded by at least twenty chairs. The servants passed their items to several butlers who placed them all on the table with an accurate eye. All lined up perfectly, there was not one speck of dust to be seen anywhere. The dishes and table gleamed and each reflected the other.

"Samantha, my child, do come and sit yourself down."

Lord Flatt approached me with arms open wide in a most amicable way, completely opposite to how I had been treated by him before. He directed me to a chair about half way down one side of the table and pulled it out for me. It reminded me of Marcus for a moment. I sat, and he helped me place it a little nearer.

"This is Master Richard Cavendish, he often visits me, deals with all my affairs involving money from the estate." He pointed another elderly gentleman out who was stood farther down the room. "He's a sort of solicitor come accountant." Both men laughed at this last statement and with both of them being rather overweight, their bellies moved and wobbled around.

Master Cavendish headed over in my direction. He took my hand and kissed it. It made me cringe. He drooled from his mouth and his breath smelt most terrible. "A pleasure to have such a pretty lady dine with us tonight, eh, Isaac?" He stared me straight in the eyes for such an unnaturally long time that I had to glance away.

"Come sit down, Richard," called Lord Flatt.

Master Cavendish squeezed my hand for a final time and smiled at me showing all his rotten teeth. I couldn't help thinking that the rest of him was rotten also. When he had taken his place, thank goodness a few chairs lower down from me, but next to Lord Flatt who sat at one end; the servants started to serve the meal. They acted it out perfectly, everyone knowing their places and lines. Not a drop of anything was spilt, and empty dishes were immediately wiped. Course after course came and went. We all sat in silence and ate, the only noises were the footsteps of the butlers as they waited on us, and the clinking of the cutlery upon the crockery. Master Cavendish ate heartily and shoved his food in like a pig at a trough. Lord Flatt ate hardly anything. He kept staring at me, which was rather unnerving, so I tried to avoid his gaze. I picked at most of my food. I ate what I recognized and the rest I just shoved around my plate to make it look like I had at least tried it. It was all too fancy for me, stuffed this, and sautéed that, all served with rich sauces and washed down with the foulest tasting of wines. The table was finally cleared and all the servants except the two men guarding me and one butler left the room, but they stood well back from the table. I continued to stare anywhere but at my two companions.

"Well, my dear," said Master Cavendish, "did you enjoy that? I certainly did." He undid the buttons on his waistcoat.

"Yes, sir, it was very nice," I replied.

"Please, call me Richard, no need for formality here, we are all friends, eh, Isaac?" Lord Flatt still sat in silence, but started to consume a large amount of the wine.

"I think that Lord Flatt is still not used to me being around," I quietly spoke.

"Lord Flatt, not used to young girls being around…that's not what I've heard." Richard laughed out loud. "Here, don't call him Lord, just Isaac will do, won't it?" and he looked directly at him for acceptance of this.

"She can call me anything she wants, but don't get used to it." He slammed the glass down onto the table. This was more the rude character that I had encountered earlier this morning. His persona seemed obviously altered with the wine, but I felt he could switch himself back and forth when it suited him any way.

"There," called Richard, "it will be just plain Isaac from now on…that's better." He gulped down a large glass of the red stuff himself, and it leaked as he drank from the corners of his mouth, running down his face. Completely unaffected by this, he just wiped his mouth and poured himself another. I cringed again. I had seen some strange characters back at the old inn, but Richard was the most pompous, odious and horrid looking. He'd was obviously a bachelor, and destined to remain one for the rest of his life. "So, Isaac, you haven't said much tonight, what did you want to see me about?"

"I want her," he scowled, "written out of my estate. Pay her off, do anything, dispose of her, anything, just get rid of her."

Well, that was a fine way to treat me on my first day here, and Richard was obviously taken aback by this statement too. He pushed himself away from the table, stood and fastened a few of the undone buttons on his waistcoat.

He commenced, "I won't beat about the bush. Normally under normal inheritance rules, the girl would not get a penny from your estate, usually passed down to the oldest surviving male line of the family. But as you have completely no other living relations of any kind, and we are talking the rules of the Flatt family, which have laws unto themselves. The property and money must go to a direct line blood descendant. I am afraid Samantha will inherit the lot except if she dies before you. Mark, your cousin, as you know, will have forfeited his inheritance as he allegedly murdered your uncle, and as he or his body has never turned up, presumed dead, the courts have passed the estate into your hands for overseeing."

"Mark murdered my uncle there is no doubt about that," yelled Isaac.

"Yes, I have heard your story, but as he has never actually been tried in a court of law the estate is not totally yours. Legally that is. Not until he is either caught, or charged, or a body turns up. Either way, with him having no relations either, Samantha will still get the lot as are the rules of the Flatt family, and they can only be possibly changed by the King himself." Richard took a deep breath as he finished speaking.

"Then I will write to the King, no way is this girl having my money." And Isaac stormed out of the room.

"What has he got against me?" I asked Richard.

"I really don't know." He shook his head. "He can be a very bitter and twisted man when he wants, he is obviously carrying a great secret around with him. I have tried to get it out of him a few times, but he just seals him self up and storms off. Over the years he has had many a young girl come and claim to be his heir. Sometimes it has taken a lot of time and money for him to prove that they are fakes. He possibly sees you as the same, but to me there is no doubt that you are genuine, as you are the double of his mother. She died when he was young and he felt betrayed. Take it from me, Samantha, it is best that we be gone when he comes back in, I've seen these moods before." He bowed and left.

I rose from my seat and my two guards instantly came to my side.

"Back to my room?" I asked. They nodded. "Am I to be constantly chaperoned?" They nodded again. "Oh well, tomorrow is another day." And I went back without any prompting.

Back at the bedroom, Sally and Jayne were there and had been warming my bed. It wasn't a particularly cold night, but their was a strong breeze building up outside and I could feel a small draft blowing in from under the window. A long white cotton nightshirt and cap had been laid out for me and they had turned the covers back on the bed. I smiled at them and they smiled back. It had been a long day for them and they looked weary.

"Who is the longest serving in the household?" I asked.

They both looked at each other for a moment and then piped up together, "Jack John."

Sally continued, "He's been here for over 40 years. He polishes and fixes the candlesticks overnight. You sometimes hear him wandering around the corridors whistling to himself, cos there is no one else around at that time of night. Master won't let him out during the day, says he is too slow and not got the right look, so he either makes himself disappear or sits in the kitchen corner. Why is that, Miss?" she asked.

"No reason. No reason at all," I said. But really I was hoping I might be able to come across some one who knew the truth, and preferably seen it with their own eyes. All I had been given was tales. The girls bid goodnight again and left. The door closed and I heard the key lock it once more.

That night I lay on my bed, half tired, but determined not to go to sleep. I had a bad feeling about this house and Isaac. I was going to wait for Jack John.

I left the curtains open in the room and the moon cast its light across all the bits and bobs and ornaments that lay around. There was an odd assortment. It looked like half belonged to a lady, brushes and pretty vases and such, and the rest to a gentleman, some sea navigation instruments and brass boxes and a small telescope. I will investigate them more thoroughly in the daylight, I told myself, incase there is anything useful to aid my escape with.

Chapter 24

Jack John

Despite my attempts to stay awake, I slept like a log that night.

The next day I heard that Isaac was going away on business for a short while, and I watched him depart through my bedroom window. He had left orders that I was to be constantly watched, but was allowed to wander around reasonably freely in the house and in the courtyard. I was not though allowed to go into the grounds.

For the next few days I strolled around the place. Although I was constantly accompanied, they slackened off a little and started to chat to me now and then. The rest of the servants in the house also seemed more at ease. Having now got used to me, they talked freely with me, not just pleasantries passing the time of day, but real issues. I guess Sally and Jayne must have told them about me, and they felt no threat.

At meal times I ate with the servants in the kitchen, there was no need to set up the dining room for one, and whilst Isaac was gone he wouldn't know what was going on. It seemed that no one was totally loyal to him, and from the kitchen banter it was evident that they all just tolerated him. He did have a couple that defended him now and then, but even they had to agree with some of the points raised about his character. One thing was obvious and that was that they all feared him. But at least while I was sitting there I ate good food, and had good conversation, which made me feel more at home.

During a few of my strolls in the courtyard, I had managed to catch a glimpse of Daniel, we waved to each other and blew a kiss. But every time I had tried to walk in his direction, I was promptly stopped by one of my guards. At least we both knew that we were alright. At nighttime I had got into the habit of viewing the sea with the telescope that I had found in my room. It was really quite powerful and looked like it had been well used. For three days there was nothing to see, but it still gave me pleasure to look. I had always had a sea view from The Four Keys and it comforted me. Then on the fourth evening I spotted a ship. Three masts, sails in full bellow, and with a red flag flying on top. It looked vaguely familiar and I watched it for quite sometime. It didn't seem to move much, and in the morning when I arose and checked—it was still there.

I dressed as usual and went down to the kitchen for breakfast. The cook had made bacon and eggs and it smelt wonderful. She had also warmed me some milk and flavored it with honey and cinnamon—her own special recipe, and it was delicious. As I sat eating, I heard a unusual disturbance at the kitchen door that led into the yard.

"Get out, you drunken fool," laughed the cook.

"But I only wants a warm and bit o'bread," came back a strong Irish accent. "Come on, dearest, won't you let your favorite man in then?"

"Alright, alright, but just you behave yourself Jack John, we have guests these days, and I don't think this young lady will be used to your sort of language, so just you mind what you says." She opened the door fully and let him in.

For a moment I thought I had seen Old Tom again. This man could have easily doubled as his twin brother from a distance. He was of the same size and build, and had the same stoop. Some of his mannerisms when he walked were the same, but now that I could clearly see his face he obviously wasn't. He was though of a similar age, but was completely clean-shaven.

He stopped and looked at me. "I've seen you before in a past life," he said which made me feel a little shivery. "You are his mother reborn, I can see why he is so angry." He took his place on a little stool in the corner near the stove. It was a very warm day already, but he still seemed to enjoy more heat. "There is no doubting you then is there." He continued to mumble something to the cook, which I didn't quite hear, but she looked at me and then back at Jack John, and agreed with whatever he had said. The cook passed him some bread and also a little butter already on knife. He spread it slowly and began to whistle to himself. He whistled a sea shanty I had heard many times before both at the inn and when Marcus had hummed it to himself when he thought I was not listening.

I continued to chew on my food, slowly, watching the cook and Jack John carefully. My guards had sat themselves down at the other end of the long kitchen table and were also having something to eat. They often let a distance get between us when they thought it safe. I edged myself closer to Jack John when they weren't watching and managed to catch a little of his conversation.

"Master is awful furious about this one," said the cook, and she continued to stir her cooking pots with her back to me. "No doubting this one though like you said, Jack."

"Aye," he replied, he glanced at me and noticed that I was watching. "Come a bit closer, child, and keep yourself warm." I moved closer and smiled at him. "Isaac a bit furious with you then?"

"Yes, he went completely mad at me a few days ago," I said.

"Aye, I heard about that. In fact I think the whole house heard it. You see, child, you have his mother's look and he is still sore from all those years ago about her dying. He had argued terrible with her, blames himself for her death; she fainted and fell down the stairs. Banged her head at the bottom just below where her picture hangs. It's a constant reminder to him, and he won't have it moved. She was wearing that very dress from the picture when it happened." He stopped talking and continued to eat his bread. The cook tutted and shook her head at him.

"Jack here had to move her body, was an awful thing to happen, such a nice lass, just like yourself, Miss," she said.

"Please call me Samantha or Sam if you like, I can't get used to this 'miss' business."

"I'll call you that when the master is not here," she replied.

"Tell me, Jack, or is it John?" I started to say.

"Either will do, Miss," he replied. "I answers to many names, some of which I can not repeat in front of your delicate ears."

Now was my chance, I had to find out about the past. “Do you remember Mark?”

“Aye, bonny looking lad.” He lowered his voice as he spoke to me. “Got robbed of his inheritance by that evil cousin of his…oww.” The cook had hit him with the ladle to shut him up.

“Don’t you be listening to Jack here, Sam, he’s a drunken fool, who tells a good tale.”

“Aye, I tells a good tale alright, but a truthful one, which is more that what Isaac can do. The lass has got to know her life is in danger if she keeps asking questions, so I am going to tell her it all now so that she can stop prying. I can see that she won’t rest until she’s convinced herself that she has got the truth.”

A very good judge of character, I thought to myself. I liked Jack John. His Irish voice suited him and entranced me as he spoke. I leaned a little closer to him, my guards where still not watching, they were too busy trying to charm one of the maids.

“No doubt Isaac’s spun you a tale about Mark killing his own father?” he commenced.

I nodded in agreement.

“Well, don’t you believe it, Sam. Mark is the nicest person I know.” A strange choice of words I thought. He spoke as though he still knew Mark was alive, everyone else always referred to him in the past dearly departed tense. “He didn’t kill him, he was forced into that room on that dreadful night to witness Isaac arguing with William. He watched Isaac strike him, and he watched him fall and hit his head on the marble table. He ran to his aid but it was too late. Covered in his father’s blood, Isaac called for help and ran locking them both in the room. Mark panicked, it was obvious what Isaac was planning to do, so he grabbed the family treasure and disappeared.”

“How do you know this?” I asked, his every word rang true with what Marcus had told me.

“I was there in the corridor tending to the candles as usual, and saw it with my own eyes through a crack in the door. When Isaac came running out, I quickly blew out the candle and hid in the dark.”

“Why haven’t you reported it then and got the true murderer hanged?”

"Well, you see the Flatt family is very powerful around here, and I am just a small fool in his employ. The local magistrate was Isaac's best friend, as is every other powerful man around these parts. His story was convincing and the evidence seemed there." He sat back and finished off the last of his bread. The cook didn't hit him this time for telling tales, and her eyes showed me that he was telling the truth.

"And the ring?" I questioned.

"Now, how did you know it was a ring that he took?" came back the reply from Jack John. He started to laugh to himself. "How did you get here? Folks say that you just turned up at Dan's cottage, but you can't just have appeared one day in a puff of smoke. Did someone bring you here? Perhaps a tall dark man who smells of the sea, with eyes bluer than the sky?" He continued to laugh and chuckle, this time so loud that everyone in the room looked at him, but then resumed their activities, thinking him a little mad.

"No," I insisted. "I made my own way here."

"And I am a monkey's uncle then." He still laughed. "Look, Sam, Isaac needs that ring to prove that you are or are not his direct blood line. All the others he has managed to pay off or get rid off, but he knows that it is more difficult with you. If you can get your hands upon it, keep hold of it tight. Don't let it out of your sight, not even when you sleep. He's a blazing about its disappearance too. I ain't going to speak about its powers, useless to me, but if you knew it could drive you mad." He leant closer to me and whispered in my ear. "I know that you've met Mark, he's told me. And I know that he's got the ring, seen the giveaway bump under his glove. He's wise to keep it covered. But if you want my advice, if he's not going to come to your rescue and get you out of here, get it from him, and wear it all the time. Isaac is adamant that he is going to destroy this family, he's tried hard for a son over the years, only for there to be nothing. And now you have come along and will waltz off with all his hard work. He's a traditional man at heart and doesn't agree with free off-loaders turning up staking a claim."

I sat upright. This Irish man had almost told me that Isaac was so bitter that if he didn't have control of the family heir line then no one would. He wanted a son, but instead had ended up with an unknown daughter. The only woman he had loved was his mother and now she was gone. He had been raised in a man's world and that was the way he wanted it to stay.

"I want to go now," I said to my guards and they came to my side.

Walking back through the long corridors, I looked at all the paintings that hung there. I hadn't noticed it before, but apart from the picture of Isaac's mother, all the rest where of men. "Which is the oldest painting in the house?" I asked my escorts.

"That will be the one in the master's private rooms," one replied.

"Can I see it? After all Isaac is not here and he did give me permission to wander freely, didn't he?" I pleaded at them by batting my eyelashes for more effect.

"This way, Miss," they said and led me to a dark room. The curtains were closed, so I went over and opened them. As I turned around, the room didn't really look very much different to any of the others. It was obviously a private drawing room and contained an assortment of chairs and tables. There were a collection of vases and various pieces of china in cupboards and other articles that you would associate with a gentleman such a pipes and spyglasses. Again several pictures hung on the walls and I glanced at them in turn.

"I am sorry, but I am not very good at reading, could you tell me which is the oldest one and what the name is written upon it?" I asked.

"It will be this one…it says…Vlad III Tepes 1431-1476, Wallachia, House of Basarab." He read it a little hesitantly probably not sure of the pronunciations of the words, they didn't sound English. They didn't mean anything to me either, but upon further examination of the picture, I could see a small silver box on a table. It was open and empty. Upon the third finger of his right hand he wore a silver ring which contained a blood red ruby type stone—just like the one that Marcus wore. There were also faintly visible several dagger-type knives one of which seemed to have been drawn partially implanted in his leg, but later roughly painted over. You could still see its outline under the paint.

As I brushed my fingers over the surface of the painting, feeling all the marks of the paint, I felt clammy and uneasy. The tips of my fingers touched the painted hand and the ring, and suddenly a breeze blew from no where through the room. It rustled some of Isaac's papers on his tables and slammed the door shut.

"These old houses always full of drafts, Miss," said one of the men and he went to close the curtains again. "Have you finished now, Miss, we really shouldn't be in here." I turned and started to walk out of the room. My eyes were still drawn to the other paintings as I passed them. I glanced at their faces; their expressions looked empty and their eyes seemed heavy and stirred out at nothing. But one thing I did notice was that each one of them wore the same ring on the same finger.

Chapter 25

The Ring Appears

For the rest of that day, I paced backwards and forwards around the house. I went several times into the courtyard, but as soon as I was there I would turn around and go back into the house. My two companions had to keep to a constant trot as I strode around impatiently. I was nervous and afraid. Isaac was due back any day. The servants had estimated that he would only return in around two weeks, but something told me that he was not going to be that long. For hours I traveled up and down the corridors of the house. I stared out of the windows as I was starting to feel uneasy about all the paintings that hung everywhere around me. Their eyes no longer seemed to stare at nothing, and always now seemed to be focused on me. In the end, my guards resorted to standing one at each end of the hallway, as they were too tired to chase me anymore. I suppose it would have been the ideal time to escape, but for some reason today it didn't cross my mind. I knew if I escaped, he would only come after me, I needed to make myself safe.

Despite my constant shifting around, I heard every footstep taken by every servant, and every tick of every clock. Their sound intensified and echoed around my head. Each new noise made me turn and look in its direction. I was beginning to feel dizzy and sick. My heart pounded faster and faster, and felt so strong that I was sure that if I glanced at my chest, I would have visibly seen it beating. Words spoken to me became fuzzy to my ears, and my eyesight started to mist over. I felt hot and shaky. Then it all started to go black. I panicked and everything around me seemed to get sucked into a long tunnel, and disappear.

When I came back to consciousness, I was lying on a chair in the dining room. Sally and Jayne were fussing over me and wafting me with some books that they had picked from a nearby bookcase. The cook was also there and my two guards.

"You gave us a right fright, my dear." The cook spoke softly and brushed bits of my hair away from my face. "Sally, go and get Miss a glass of cold water."

Sally left immediately. I tried to raise myself up, but was held down by the cook. "Just wait until Sally is back, get your coordination back first before you get up. Been out for nearly 15 minutes, Miss. Ahh...here she is."

Sally dashed back in spilling some of the water on the floor, which was mopped up instantly by Jayne. I took a small sip aided by the cook and tired to sit up again. I still felt a little dizzy but seemed to be calmer.

"Don't know what came over you then, Miss. Gave us a terrible panic. You dropped on the floor at exactly the same spot as the master's mother did, for a moment we thought you were dead, you went as white as sheet, and were as cold as marble to touch...even sent for your brother. Here he is now." The cook had spotted him through the window running across the courtyard.

I turned my head in the direction of the running footsteps to see Daniel dashing towards me.

"Sammy, Sammy," he called, and it sounded good to me to hear him. "Are you alright? They told me you were ill, probably even dead of fright. Thank goodness you are alright." He grabbed my hand and held it tight. "I could not have coped if you had gone." His eyes started to fill with tears. Gently I wiped them away, just like he had done for me, and smiled at him.

"Well, as you can see I am all still here," I quipped, making light of the situation. "Take more than a fainting spell to get rid of me."

He grabbed me strongly and pulled me to his chest. I flung my arms around him and we squeezed each other for comfort. It was good to hold him, and it made me feel a little shaky again, but this time differently. We pulled apart and our eyes met. I had never noticed what beautiful eyes he had before. A different kind of feeling towards him filled my body, and I started to blush. He smiled back at me give me a gentle kiss on the cheek. It was soft and sweet, and I knew that I would remember its tingling touch forever. I wanted him to hold me again, but he pulled away, I think a little embarrassed himself.

"If you ever need me, just tell Jack John and he'll get in touch," he said.

I needed him now, but understood the situation and let him go. But before he went, I grabbed him and whispered in his ear, "Is Marcus about? Tell him I need to get away from here. He'll know what to do."

Daniel stood up, nodded to me in a sort of bowing way to try not to make it obvious, and ran out of the room the same way as he had come in. I watched him go and wished that I could have gone with him.

The rest of the servants fussed over me for some time. I let them do it, although annoying and unnecessary it kept my mind busy and away from thoughts of danger. Eventually they went back to their chores and I was left sat in the room on my own. Even my guards had stepped out to give me some space. It became the opposite of the hustle and bustle that had just taken place and went eerily quiet. I felt the same sudden chilling breeze that had brushed by in Isaac's private rooms, but looking out the window I could see that the trees were perfectly still, so put it down to just one of those drafts that you get around old houses.

I decided to skip dinner that evening and retired to bed early. The sun had just set and the moon was starting to rise, bathing everything with its pale light. I changed into my bedclothes and stood by the window. It made few of the servants in the courtyard jump when they saw me there. Dressed all in white, I looked like a ghost at the window, and I could hear them commenting on how much I looked like Isaac's mother Alice, and how for a moment they thought she had returned again. Again? What did they mean by that? I moved away from the window and knocked on my bedroom door loudly so that the guards would open it. Bill, the taller of the two, swore quite profusely when he saw me stood there. The moonlight shone upon me making my complexion look very pale and the breeze from the opening door caused my clothes and hair to blow a little.

"I am most sorry, Miss, I didn't mean to say that." Bill apologized most humbly. "Just you standing there and your clothes and that…well, it was as though the master's ghost had returned."

"What do you mean? I didn't mean to scare you I only wondered if I could get some water to drink, my throat is little dry." I didn't really want any, but felt that I had to justify why I wanted the door opening.

"Yes, Miss, that's fine, I will go and get some for you."

"No," I stopped him. "I would like to go for it myself. I promise that I will come back. After all, I can't run away in a night dress, can I?" I smiled at him.

"I don't think it's right…but seeing as I have come over a little faint myself…I don't suppose on this occasion it would do any harm. You haven't given us any reason for concern so far, been a perfect captive. But I shall be counting, I know how long it takes to get to the kitchen and back, and if you ain't back here in three minutes, I am assuming you missing."

"I don't like it, Bill," spoke my other guard.

"Argh, she'll behave herself, don't you worry, too much at stake with this one," Bill answered back, and reluctantly they both let me go. I hitched up my nightdress to my knees, and ran barefoot as fast as I could down the corridor and down the main staircase. I was not afraid of the dark, nor of any ghost tales, I had heard too many of them from The Four Keys to let them bother me. There was always a reason behind why something happened, well that was my theory!

Being barefoot I made little to no noise as I hastily went in the direction of the kitchen. Part way down the corridor I could hear singing coming from one of the rooms. It sounded as though some of the servants were having a little get together and a bit of fun whilst their master was away. I whipped my way past their door and continued on my journey. It was getting darker down this end of the house. There were fewer candles casting their dancing shadows on the walls. I stopped for a moment to catch my breath and it was here that I heard a sea shanty being whistled. Jack John, I thought to myself. I know…if anyone knew about ghostly going ons it would be him, after all he traveled the house at night when most ghosts are supposed to come out.

Stepping into the shadows, I waited until he came around the corner and a little nearer to me.

"Jack," I whispered softly. He stopped, listened and then shook his head. "Jack," I whispered again.

"Who be it? Make yourself know to Jack John then." He raised his candle snuffer up into the air in a defensive position, and held his own candle a little nearer to his face supposedly to give him more light to see, but all it did was highlight his wrinkles.

"It's me," I quietly called back and stepped out into what light there was.

"Mother of Jesus…God save us…it's…it's…" He staggered a little.

"It's me," I said again. "Sam."

"Saints be praised, child. You nearly had me dead and cold then." He sat down on a nearby chair and patted his heart with his hand. "Mind you, I nearly had you dead and cold as well. I ain't afraid of anything that comes to me in the night." And he waved his snuffer around.

"Yes, you look like you aren't." I laughed.

"What on earth are you doing out and about down here?" he asked.

"Just came for some water," I replied.

"Don't you know you have servants to do that sort of thing for you?"

"Yes, but I also was secretly hoping that I would bump into you as well."

Jack John calmed down. "Well, now you have found me, ask away, no doubt you have some question to ask me."

"Yes, I have. I heard this evening that Isaac's mother is a ghost these days. Is it true?" I stared at him straight in the eyes so that he knew I would spot if he told a lie.

"No, it ain't true. Well, at least in as much as no one has ever seen her. Plenty say that they have felt her though blowing around the place looking for Isaac. Chilly breezes when you don't expect one and that sort of thing. Isaac swears blind that he's actually seen her several times, and it's sort of put us all on edge a little, but he does drink alot. Do me a favor, Sam, and next time you wants to wander around at night, take a candle and wear some different clothes." Jack John got up and straightened himself.

"I've got to get back now," I said, "my guards have let me out on trust, don't want to ruin my chances of getting away from them again sometime." With that I turned and ran back to my room. The guards were getting a little uneasy with my absence and were starting to shift around a bit, but relaxed when they saw me come back.

Safely locked back in my room, I lay on my bed and thought. I couldn't get to sleep, as the night was hot. Where was Alice when you needed a cool breeze? Perhaps my likeness to his mother could work to my advantage. If I played my cards right and tried to start to warm to Isaac a little, he might start to accept me. If not I could always pretend haunt him in the night!

After a while I did start to drift into sleep. Half gone I could still vaguely hear footsteps outside my door and a sea shanty being whistled—no doubt Jack John on his rounds. I rolled over on my bed and hid my head under my pillow to completely deaden the noise. But it didn't go away, and for a moment seem to only get a lot louder. I sat up and stared at my door, only to see a small package being pushed underneath. I rose and picked it up and being very puzzled opened it. Inside I found —the ring. Clutching it tightly in my hand, I listened to the whistling dwindle away, only to hear it come back again a few minutes later. The pitch of it sounded a little different though, and this time the footsteps seemed to give away a shuffle, which had not been there before. This second walk was obvious that of Jack John, but the first had been clear and precise. The steps had been firm and intentional. It suddenly dawned upon me…the ship I could see out at sea…the comments that Jack John had made…the request I had sent with Daniel…my first visitor, my gift giver had to have been Marcus.

Chapter 26

Isaac Returns

I clutched the ring tightly. This was it. If Marcus had sent me the ring, he must know that my life was in danger, he didn't part lightly with this treasured possession. I started to scramble around the room, looking for a place to hide it. If I had worn it on my finger it would have been blatantly obvious to everyone that I had got it, and besides it was too large for me so I may have lost it. Finally, I came across a box containing a selection of chains. Searching amongst them I came across a rather long gold necklace which would suit. I looped it around and through the ring so that there was no way it could possibly fall off and placed it over my head. It hung low against my chest. Good, I thought I could wear this and tuck the ring safely inside my dress away from prying eyes. I lay awake for the rest of the night, not letting go of the ring. Fears traveled through my mind and body, and I dreaded the coming of the next day, but it came sooner than expected.

As my clock struck seven, each chime echoed slowly around the room. Suddenly there was a knock at the door, my heart stopped for a moment. But to my relief it was followed by the voices of Sally and Jayne, they had just come to aid my dressing as usual. The guards let them in and with them they brought a reassuring wave of noise as they constantly chatted about this and that. The sun was up and the day looked brighter. I felt calmer.

I kept the ring out of their sight and got dressed behind the screen. They had laid me out a beautiful dress in the palest of pink colors. I had only ever dreamed of owning such items when I was young, and now here I was wearing them all day long. They weren't very practical for climbing and running, but it didn't matter, as I wasn't given the chance to do any. The chain hung perfectly across my chest and hid the ring below the bust line. The girls commented on how pretty a necklace it was and I thanked them for their kind comments. Then I began my daily routine of first visiting the kitchen for some breakfast.

Breakfast today was porridge sweetened with honey. It was lovely and gave me a warm feeling inside. After I had finished I thanked the cook, who was the only one present, and proceeded to one of the drawing rooms. My guards sat themselves down, something they would not have done had Isaac been here, and let me wander around freely. I looked at all the books and even took a few from the shelves. Unable to read them I felt a little inferior, but most of them had some pictures in them so I could imagine what they were about. There were hundreds of them in this particular room, most bound in either red or brown leather, with gold writing and neat patterns down their spines.

"Looks like we are in for some bad weather," said one of the men and gestured with his hand to one of the windows as we both looked towards him. Sure enough large dark clouds were slowly covering the perfect blue of the day. As I looked I could see the trees were starting to sway and the pheasants and deer all returning to their shelters. This was the first bit of bad weather I had seen in a long time. Now I wouldn't even be able to go into the courtyard for some fresh air, and it was boring enough being in the house!

I sat myself down by the men and watched the sky rapidly blacken. Several other servants dashed in and out of the room lighting extra candles to brighten the darkening room. Then the rain came. It streamed from the sky. The drops so heavy the wind could only just manage to move them and lash them against the windows. It was relentless, and large puddles soon appeared in the over perfect courtyard. What seemed to be two gardeners, ran across the grounds and I could see that they were going to get soaked to the bone. The raindrops running down the window obscured their faces, but I hoped that one wasn't Daniel.

Then unexpectedly a footman shouted out, "Master's back, master's back." All hell seemed to let loose within the house. My guards instantly jumped to their feet and stood beside me. There was the sound of horse's hooves outside and some more voices, as the liverymen came to their aid. I heard a banging on the main doors and Isaac shouting, "Open." The doors swung wide apart and the wind blew Isaac and the rain inside. Thunder rumbled as he stomped along the corridor towards the drawing room, and the wind outside was starting to howl. I could hear him casting off wet articles of clothing as he headed in my direction, his gloves, his hat and his riding coat, and his butler running behind him picking them up from the floor. Lightning flashed and in the intensity of the moment it made me gasp. As the flash subsided, Isaac loomed large at the drawing room door and stared straight at me. Deep hatred was in his dark eyes. He was without his usual wig, and the rain dribbled miserably down what was left of his real hair and dripped in slow motion onto his shoulders and then the floor. His hands were clenched into tight fists and he still carried his riding whip.

"I will not have this woman take my hard work from me," he announced to all. "I was weak before when I first saw her. Tricks of the light only make her look like my mother. She does not convince me. I will prove her a fake like all the others. As God is my witness, I will die penniless before she gets one ounce of my money." Isaac turned and headed back up the corridor to be met by Richard Cavendish, who had by his attire been obviously accompanying Isaac on his journey.

"Now don't do anything foolish, Isaac…Isaac…listen to me, Isaac, we can sort this out." Richard scurried after him and followed him when he went into his private chambers. The door slammed shut and I could hear Isaac blazing inside. Obviously his journey to see the King had been a waste of time. After several long minutes Richard came out looking rather sheepish and passed his wet riding attire to one of the servants. A fire had been started in the great entrance hall and Richard went and stood by it to dry off the remainder of his clothes. A servant brought him a glass of brandy and he downed it in one, dribbling as usual, and wiping his mouth with his sleeve. I remained in the relative safety of the drawing room until early evening, but watched all the time through the open door.

It had rained persistently all day long. Everything was very wet and very damp. Thunder rumbled around as though unable to find in the sky its final resting place, only to be disturbed in its journey by a stab of lightning now and then. My stomach was just starting to rumble as well, from hunger, when Sally came in.

"Master has instructed that you should accompany him for dinner tonight." Seeing that I looked worried, she added in a quiet whisper, "Don't worry, Miss, Master Richard Cavendish will be there as well, so you won't be on your own with him." She gave me a friendly wink. I forced a smile out for her, and headed toward the dining room.

Richard and Isaac were already seated when I entered, in exactly the same chairs as last time. Richard acknowledged my presence and stood until I was seated myself. Isaac didn't even look at me. We were served the whole of the meal, all four courses, in absolute silence. Only the clanging of the cutlery or the chinging of the china was to be heard again. My previous state of hunger had some how completely disappeared, and I seemed to only push most of my food around my plate.

"Well, this is a fine to do," said Richard, breaking our silence. "I could have got a better conversation from the corpse at the morgue than from you two." He tried feebly to make some light conversation.

"Yes," I replied, "but the food wouldn't have been as good!" We both laughed politely.

"Funny, is it?" Finally Isaac spoke. "Funny, is it? My hospitality? I will tell you what is funny." He rose and started to circle the table. "Funny is the number of girls that I have had at my door over the years, claiming to be my daughter. Funny is that you, Richard, my so-called best friend can't help me to get rid of this one. Funny is the way she resembles my mother. Funny is the way she comes in through my front door and tries to take my fortune away. Funny is the way that I am going to get rid of her." He suddenly stopped behind me.

I didn't like this last sentence. He leaned over me and breathed hard as he forced his words out. "What is this then, Samantha?" He touched my neck with his fingers and stroked it over my chest. My heart pounded, and he flicked out the necklace onto my dress revealing the ring.

"It's…it's…is that it?" choked Richard on his drink.

"Oh, yes, Richard, it is the very one indeed." Isaac's eyes flashed with the fire of greed. The same look that I had seen on the pirates when they realized that Marcus had the ring. "How did you come to get this then?"

"I found it," I said.

"I don't believe you. You are a little thief, stole it from someone I bet."

"No, no, look I can prove who I really am now." I slipped the ring from its chain and placed it upon my third finger of my right hand. I stood and waved my hand around in front of him.

"That doesn't prove anything, anyone can wear the ring. But this will prove it." He turned away from me and headed toward the fireplace.

"Now, Isaac, don't be rash, don't do anything you will regret," stuttered Richard, getting a little flustered.

"I am certainly not going to regret this," he hissed out and swung around to reveal a loaded pistol in his hand pointed directly at me.

Chapter 27

My End

The shot hit me with such force that it knocked me off my feet. As I fell backwards in what seemed like an unreal situation, I could see the smile upon his face, and the panic upon Richard. It was at first like I had been hit hard in the stomach and it winded me. My arms and legs were flung upwards, and I must have looked like a rag doll that had been thrown by a child. I hit the floor with much force and crumpled. Then I felt a warm sensation flow over me and as I looked down at my dress, I could see that I was bleeding heavily. My blood soaked into the material in an ever-increasing circular pattern. I felt no pain—I was in shock.

"There, I told you that she was no relative of mine," smirked Isaac, and calmly placed the pistol back on top of the fireplace.

Richard came running to my aid, as did the other servants that were present in the room.

"Isaac, you fool. I can't believe that you have just done this. I didn't think you so low as to take another's life for your own interest," Richard said.

"Then you really don't know me at all," he replied, and he carefully took himself a drink from a nearby table.

But what I couldn't understand was why my life was pouring out of me when I wore the ring. The ring that I had been led to believe was the savior of life. I glanced at my hand only to see the ring not there. The force of the blast had knocked me backwards and caused the ring, which was a loose fit on me, to fly through the air and roll away. I was doomed, I could feel myself starting to go dizzy, this was to be my end.

As I lay there, the room started to swirl. Richard held tight onto my hand and shouted at some of the servants to get some clean linen so that he could press it into my wound. Outside the thunder still rolled and the lightning flashed. I felt a cold breeze blow over me and thought that maybe it was Alice, coming to take me away. But it came instead this time from an opened door. As I gazed around, I could barely make out the outlines of two men stood there, but still I recognized them.

"Daniel," I screamed. "Help me."

"Sammy," he yelled back and rushed to my side. "Hold on, Sammy, I am here for you, I will help you, just hold on, Sammy."

But in his face I could see that he knew the situation helpless. He rose to his feet, and with anger etched into his voice called to Isaac, "I am going to kill you." Grabbing for a knife from his belt, he lunged at Isaac, but he dodged.

"Don't waste your time with him, Dan, find the ring." The second man spoke; it was Marcus. Now fully into the room everyone there could see him clearly. "Find the ring, Dan; it can save her," he yelled. "I will take care of Isaac." He pulled out his sword and held it against Isaac's throat. As Daniel searched furiously around the room, he was joined by Sally and Jayne. Finally he found it, and back at my side placed it upon my third finger.

"Sammy, darling, it's going to be alright, I have found it." But I didn't feel the same. I had lost so much blood; my faith in it had gone. Isaac, despite having a blade at his throat, still drank his wine and watched with amusement the entertainment.

"Even if she was my child, it's too late now," he mused.

"No, no I won't have it, it's never too late," called back Daniel.

"Look, sir, look, sir," said Sally, "the blood has stopped flowing. It's true. It's true."

"Or she may just be dead," chipped in Isaac. "Blood can't flow if the heart has stopped beating." Isaac was growing impatient with the situation "Clear her body away, it's of no use to me, Daniel, you may have it." He wafted his handkerchief in my direction, then patted his lips to dry them from the wine.

"Isaac, this action is beyond the call of reality. It has no sense. You will be hanged for this. All these people, and I am afraid to say, I included, will bear witness to it." Richard, despite his ogre-like character, was the voice of sense and reason.

"That is, those of you who are not afraid to speak against me." Isaac pushed Marcus's blade away from him and took a step backwards.

Richard still clutched my hand. "The poor child," he started to say when he noticed my chest move. "Wait, wait…she is still breathing, she is coming round. Samantha, do you know what happened to you?" He implored me to answer.

"Yes…er…a shot…Isaac…a gun," my speech was a little broken. Daniel ripped my dress open at my stomach where the shot had entered and all persons present were taken aback. The wound was visible, but it was not bleeding and was in fact part healed.

"No doubt that she is your child now. A true blood descendant of the family," spoke Marcus.

"I lay no claim to her," he scowled. "I was tricked by her whore of a mother. And I lay no claim to you either, Mark." He bent swiftly and drew a hot poker from the fire and crossed it against Marcus's blade.

A gasp went up from around the room. Many of the servants had been at the house for a long time, but none of them had recognized Mark. They had just seen a rough-looking pirate sort come in with Daniel. With the commotion that was already going on, no one had bothered to ask him who he was.

"Aye, that be Mark alright," said an Irish voice from the doorway.

"Good to see you again, Jack," called Marcus lightly heartedly.

"Like wise," he called back. "Just you set the records straight now."

Chapter 28
The Fight for Truth

Isaac rubbed his poker slowly up and down Marcus' blade, taunting him and also edging him away slowly from the fireplace. His face carried a smirk of content; he wasn't about to let Marcus get the better of him.

"While you have been away, dear cousin, thieving, robbing and drinking, and all those other filthy activities that you pirates do, I have been growing wise. I would lay my life on it that you have only stayed alive so long because of the ring."

"Then lay your life on it, and I will fight you blade to blade without the ring, and right my father's death," Marcus replied. He stepped back and allowed Isaac to reach for one of the ornamental, but real, blades on the wall. The servants all quickly departed to safety, but Richard and Daniel stayed by my side. Isaac, in his usual double crossing way, removed two blades instead of just the one offered.

He lunged at Marcus with both blades, who luckily managed to quickly deflect them both and run to the other side of the table were there was more room for battle.

"Is that all you can do, Mark, run away?" chortled Isaac.

"Well, it is better to live than die, but all the better with a clear conscience," replied Marcus.

"If you are referring to things of the past, I forgive you."

"Forgive me?" said Marcus. "It is you that needs forgiveness, so beg for mercy from your Lord before I put you into hell to suffer from your own actions."

"I'll see you in there first," Isaac called back and ran around the table to meet Marcus.

Despite carrying extra weight, Isaac was quite nimble on his feet, and his bladesmanship was excellent. However, Isaac had been taught to fence by a tutor and not ever had to do it for real to save his life—unlike Marcus. His footwork was impeccable but not crafty enough to stay ahead. The blades clashed and swirled with ferocious speed. Each lunge was equally matched by another, and despite Isaac having the use of two blades, it initially seemed like Marcus was playing with him. Marcus leaped around, hiding behind chairs, jumping over stools and even rolled over the table to dodge him. Isaac just could not make any mark upon him.

Furious, he growled at Marcus. "Stand still and fight like a man not a leaping demon."

"If that is the way you prefer, then who am I not to oblige." Marcus stopped his dancing around. He was used to darting in and out of riggings, and vaulting over onto attackers ships, but now he stood his ground firm and hardly moved. The blades continued to encounter with rapacious force. Isaac was starting to sweat, grabbing at his wig; he threw it at Marcus. It knocked Marcus' swing out of time and Isaac managed to slash his arm.

"Ahh, first strike to me, I believe," smiled Isaac, still raining blows down.

"A lucky shot, that is all, you won't get another chance, the next blood to flow will be yours." Marcus was obviously in some pain as he winced, and despite his promise to stand still, he darted away from the onslaught.

"Daniel, quick give him the ring," I said and pulled it from my finger. I was no longer in any need of it as my wound had completely healed. Daniel took it and started to head towards Marcus.

"No, Dan, I don't want it. I promised an equal fight, and I am a man of my word." Marcus winced again as he spoke, and Daniel respected his wishes and stood back.

"I told you that you had only survived for so long because of the ring, didn't I? And this proves it. Some fine pirate you turned out to be. What did you end up as, ships cook? Carpenter? Cabin boy?" Isaac laughed. His mockery burned in Marcus' soul.

Marcus pulled himself upright ignoring the pain, and replied proudly, "Captain actually, of a fine fleet of ships I am."

"Small fishing boats, catching local crabs and whiting no doubt," sneered Isaac.

That was it, hatred blazed in Marcus. He bombarded Isaac with a battalion of blows. So hard and mad, that Isaac lost one of his blades, and was left to desperately try and defend himself with the other. Marcus now had regained the upper hand.

"This one is for my father," he called, and savagely struck down with his blade. "And this one is for my aunt." He laid his blade down hard against Isaac's again.

Petrified, Isaac spoke hurriedly, "That one was an accident, she fell…she fell…you have to believe me, she fell." With tears starting to well in his eyes, remembering his mother, Isaac started to whimper. Marcus stepped away and watched Isaac fall to the floor and sob like a small child. "That was an accident…please…please…if I could turn back time, I would." He held his hands in a clasped praying position and pleaded with Marcus to believe him.

"Aye, well, I didn't see it happen, but I did hear you argue with her which no doubt brought on her fainting spells. Where as I did see you hit my father." Marcus stared hard at Isaac. This was too easy to kill him. He was defenseless, as he had laid down his blade. Now Marcus had the perfect chance for revenge, he wandered whether he should do it. Was it really worth it? So many years had gone by. Blood had already been shed in the house, was it to see some more? The rain was still heavy outside and the thunder and lightning still rolled around and speared the sky. A sudden gust blew open one of the large windows and it caught us all by surprise. Marcus for a second glanced away from Isaac and at the billowing curtains. It was all Isaac needed. He grasped his blade from the floor and swiftly thrust it into Marcus's back. This time when the blade was withdrawn, it was covered with blood. I screamed and buried my face into Richard's chest. This was not supposed to happen. The blood was pouring from him and dripping onto the polished floor.

Marcus turned and looked at Isaac in disbelief. He was laughing. He stood there laughing.

"You should not have done that," spoke Marcus softly.

"Why what are you going to do about it?" chuckled Isaac.

"This," said Marcus, and he drew one of his pistols and shot Isaac squarely in the chest from close range. "Now who is laughing?"

Isaac was speechless. His blood now poured from his wound, and joined Marcus' on the polished floor. Like two crimson snakes becoming one, the bloods merged together creating a lake of death. They stood there looking at each other, each not believing what the other had done. Then I remembered again the ring.

"Dan, the ring, the ring, throw it to them."

He did.

It sailed through the air, spinning, and glinting in the candlelight. They both reached for it together and seemed both to grab it. Weakened from the blood loss, they both fell to the floor with their fists tightly clenched. But who had got it?

Richard, Daniel and I, ran to the other side of the table to see both men lying there. They were motionless, face down in their own blood. We stood shocked, and watched their bodies—there was nothing we could do.

The wind howled outside again and blew the curtains through the open window. Richard, ever practical, strode over to close it, but didn't make the full distance. He froze on the spot half way, and as we looked, we saw the outline of a woman walking in the courtyard. She was dressed all in white with a very pale complexion. Despite the persistent rain, she seemed unaffected, completely dry. She turned in the direction of the opened window and she looked very familiar. She walked into the dining room silently, and headed over toward the two bodies. Kneeling at the side of Isaac, we realized who she was. It was the ghost of Alice, Isaac's mother. So she was real. She stroked his hair and kissed his hand lovingly, but then unexpectedly plunged her hand violently into his body. When she withdrew it, she brought out with her his soul. His very image rose out of his body. He seemed to be startled and unaware of what was happening, but then he saw her and he started to sob. But her kind face altered, and her ghostly flesh fell away to reveal her maggot-eaten skeleton, as she would truly look after so long in the grave. Isaac started to protest that he didn't do it, but it was useless, he was in her hands now. She pulled his soul across the room and back out of the window, and across the courtyard from where she had come.

Shaking, Richard rushed to the window, slammed it shut and drew the curtains across. There was still another body in the room; he didn't want to experience that again.

But he need not have worried. As Daniel rolled Marcus' body over, there was a small groan. His right hand was still clenched tight, but as he peeled back his fingers, he could see that the ring was partially placed upon his finger.

Chapter 29

Departure

Wisely, the loyal servants put us all to bed for rest,, and I slept truly good. When the morning came, I felt completely healed. A little sore maybe, but no more than if I had taken a good punch to the ribs area and was suffering bruising. As I opened my eyes, Sally and Jayne were there in my room fussing about as usual. Daniel was also there. He held my hand. I smiled at him, and he gently smiled back at me.

"I'll leave you to get dressed now." He spoke softly and pulled his hand away from mine as he rose, and he walked backwards out of the room not taking his glances away from my happy face.

"Ooh, he's a darling, Miss. If I knew he had been here at the estate all along, I would have been making him my sweetheart before now," chuckled Jayne, and Sally nodded in agreement.

"He's not my sweetheart…he's my brother and…" And I was going to say that that was all, but then I remembered that he was not really my brother at all.

"Whatever you say, Miss, but I should like to see one of my brothers sit beside my bed all night and hold my hand like what he did," replied Sally. I guess I must have blushed awfully as both girls broke out into streams of unstoppable giggles.

"Marcus, where is Marcus?" I quickly remembered, after I had calmed a little. "Is…"

"He is alright, Miss. He's in the next room getting some rest. Jack John been watching him all night, but I dare say he would have preferred a prettier face to do it, but beggars cant be choosers," said Jayne, and she handed me some clothes to put on. "Now if you don't mind, Miss, in light of last night's events, you need to get dressed and come down stairs quickly."

I did what I was told.

Downstairs, Richard was waiting. He was still visibly shaken from the experience, but pleased to see me. "I have had what is left of Isaac laid out in one of the spare stables until the undertakers arrive. I didn't think you would want him left in the house," he said.

"You did right, Richard. I am afraid I misjudged you when I first met you and would like to apologize for my silence towards you." I offered my hand out to him to hold.

He took them briefly and replied, "That's alright, Samantha. I have spent too much time in the company of Isaac and lost touch with the real world around me. If you would kindly let me serve you, I would be pleased to continue to manage the estate accounts. Isaac lost me most of my other clients due to his behavior."

"That would be very nice. Thank you, Richard, at least I don't have to worry about them now for a while." I smiled at him and he seemed to stop his shaking a little. I think he was just as frightened of me rejecting his offer this morning as he was of the events of last night. He was a little washed up in his financial world, and had obviously lost some of his credibility.

Suddenly, there was a violent knocking at the main door. One of the doormen answered it, and we saw him being rudely pushed to one side, as several rough-looking men forced their way in despite his protests.

"Miss Samantha Flatt?" one of them bellowed. It seemed strange to hear myself being called this name.

"That is I," I replied, and stepped forward.

"I am the Crown's Officer and believe that you were involved in a serious crime last night."

"Do I look like I have been involved in any serious crimes?" I inquired.

"That is not for me to say," he snapped back. "My men have a warrant and a right to search these premises for evidence regarding the murder of Master Isaac Flatt by one named Mark Flatt or Marcus

Fleet, wanted on several previous accounts of murder and piracy."

I was taken aback, and in an attempt to delay their search stated bluntly, "No, I do not give you permission to invade my private residence," and stood in front of them.

"It's not up to you, Miss," and he waved for the men to split and commence their duties.

They pushed the servants aside, who had heard the commotion, and were doing their best to get in their way, and started to hunt downstairs. After a few minutes of feverish pillaging, they found nothing. To my surprise even the dining room had not a single trace of anything having been out of place.

"Upstairs," one called and they all began to head towards the main staircase.

"I really must protest…this is not at all on…Richard, can they do this?" I asked.

"I am afraid they can, Samantha. It would appear that some of Isaac's loyaler servants ran to the village last night and reported the unnatural events, and it's their duty to check it all out," he replied helplessly.

"No, I won't have it." I rushed up the stairs and got ahead of the men. "This is my house and there is nothing to report. Isaac was drunk and slipped…and…and…shot himself accidentally." I acted out the shooting to try and elaborate my story, but they were not falling for it, and knocked me aside. In desperation, I tried again to get ahead of them, especially when they came to the bedroom where Marcus was lying. They tried to open the door, but it had been locked from the inside.

"Who is in here, Miss?" the officer asked.

"No one," I replied, trying to sound all innocent.

"Then why is it locked, are you hiding someone?"

"No.. er…the key got lost last week by one of the maids…when…er…she was cleaning the room." My words fumbled and tumbled out of my mouth. I hoped this had sounded convincing, but he just looked at me and then proceeded to smash the door down with his shoulder. It took him only two attempts and he was in. I held my breath as he entered, and then released it with relief when he came back out and grunted ,"The beds still warm but there is no one there. Better keep an eye on those servants, Miss. Either you is lying, or they are having you over. To the courtyard men, search everywhere." They scattered and left me in peace for the moment.

I stood there confused. Where had he gone? Daniel appeared.

"Dan, where has he gone?" I whispered.

"Don't worry, Jack John heard them coming and has taken him out the back way. He locked the door to delay them a little while he hid him. They won't find him. Now go back downstairs and act normal in case they come back." He pushed me in the direction of the stairs and then casually followed me a few steps behind to make it look like we were unconnected.

After 15 minutes the officer and his men came back to my door. "I don't know where he is hiding, Miss, but from the state that he is reported to have been in, the only place he can hide now is in a grave. You haven't heard the last from me. I know there is something going on." And with that he reluctantly left.

I gladly closed the door, and all the servant came around me, most breaking house rules and giving me a gentle pat on the shoulder in both a comforting and well-done manner before they resumed their daily tasks.

"Thank you, thank you, everyone," I called to them as they left me, Richard and Daniel stood there.

"If you would excuse me, Samantha, I have paperwork to get on with. My eyes have been opened last night to Isaac's true character, and I don't want to get involved with Mark. I will leave him in the capable hands of his aides, but you can trust me to keep my own silence," said Richard, and he hurriedly left the building, throwing a brief wave as he closed the door behind him.

I looked at Daniel and he looked at me, and we both hugged each other in relief. "So where is Marcus now?" I asked.

"Come and see," said Daniel and he led me back upstairs to the bedroom. "Jack John has brought him back in, safest place for him to be is back inside again now."

As we got the bedroom, I could see through the open door, Marcus sitting up in bed. He was naked to the waist and I could now see his full fleet of ships. Very impressive, I thought.

"Sam, come in, my dear, I am as good as new now," he said, and twisted around so that I could see his healed wound.

"That's as maybe," said Jack John, "but you lost a lot of blood before you managed to get that damned ring on. You gave us all a fright, thought we had lost you."

"It will take more than that to get rid of me. I intend to live forever." Marcus smiled, showing his sparkling white teeth. You would have never known from the condition of his hair, teeth and skin, that he had spent nearly 15 years at sea, living on the edge. Put him in some different clothes and he would really fit the perfect image of a fine country gentleman. But he was a pirate in the country. A country pirate, you could say.

I didn't ask how he had got in and out of the building without a trace, I was just glad to see him.

"Now Samantha, getting down to some serious business. Now that Isaac is gone, there is no one to dispute the blood inheritance of the estate. Due to my change of career from landowner to ship owner, I am unable to stay safely on shore. So I give the estate and all the land to you to look after." He hauled himself out of bed and started to get dressed. He was looking a little weak, but he was still alive.

"I don't want it. It's not mine. It's rightfully yours," I protested.

"You are not listening to me, Samantha. As much as I have longed to return to my home and walk freely amongst the pheasants and the deer, I can never do it. I have not lead a good life at sea and have disposed of a few people, in shall we say, a rather unpleasant way. I have written a letter of transference, which is still valid despite my behavior, and stated clearly in it that you being of the Flatt blood must inherit."

Fully dressed, he looked for his hat, which he found and placed neatly upon his head. Jack John passed him his arrangement of guns and knifes, and his image was now as complete as it was on the first day that I had met him. "Richard is a honest man, really, I have known about him for many years. Isaac's deep pocket and a good life easily led him, but he will sort you out and manage your finances fine. Let him worry about it for a while."

Marcus headed towards me. He placed his hands upon mine and pressed the ring into my palm. "You must look after this now."

"I don't want it," I stated bluntly. "It has already brought more blood shed than I can bear in the short time that I have known about it. Take it to sea with you, you will need it more than me."

"No, you must have it, to pass on," he insisted.

"No, Marcus, I won't have it. If you don't want it, throw it into the sea, let this be the end of a bad family tradition. I have already broken the line by being the first female to inherit, let's start something new."

The ring sparkled as I stared at it in my hand. The blood red ruby's cloudy complexion seemed to move and clear to a brighter hue. A trick of the light no doubt, as where I stood the sun shone brightly upon me from an opened window.

"You really don't know what power you have in your hand, do you, Sam?" said Marcus. "It contains the blood of this family both in it and on it. But…if you really don't want to keep it, I suppose I could use it a little more…and return it at a later date." A glint of mischief shone in his eyes and his mouth curled into a curious little smile. He placed the ring upon his finger and then put on his black gloves. "Besides, you have some family blood of your own to sort out." He nodded in Daniel's direction. "Take care of her, Dan." And with that he turned and left the room. A curious draught of air seemed to follow his direction that caused the bedding and curtains to blow a little for a few seconds after he had gone.

I left the room where he had been resting and returned to my own bedchamber. As I looked out of my window down onto the courtyard, I could see Marcus mounting a horse. It was true, he couldn't have stayed here. He waved his hat at me, and I waved back. Then he rode the horse magnificently out of the courtyard and down the long lane to the gate near Daniel's old house. His country skills had never really left him.

Far out at sea, I could see his ship waiting to whisk him away, to wreck havoc upon some unsuspecting sailors for some rum and a bit of gold, like all pirates do. No doubt though he would be back when I least expected it.

Printed in the United Kingdom
by Lightning Source UK Ltd.
107280UKS00002B/1-51